W

"A wee...   a exclaimed.   ...hardly believe it. It's a dream date—you absolutely,
positively have to go!"

When Katie didn't say anything, Melissa
stared at her. "You *are* going, aren't you?"

"How can I, when I'm going steady with
Scott?" Katie said. "Unless he says it's okay,
that is. I'm going to tell him about it
tomorrow."

Melissa groaned. "You have to be out of
your mind, Katie Jean O'Connor! Scott will
never agree to your spending an entire weekend with some other guy, even if he's just
your brother's roommate. He'll never understand that something like this isn't a real
date—it's an *event*! You can't tell him about
it, you just can't."

"I guess I'll have to think about it some
more," Katie said. "Now let's tackle that trig
assignment, okay? Compared to my problem, it ought to be a piece of cake!"

Recent Bantam titles in the Sweet Dreams series. Ask your bookseller for titles you have missed:

WEEKEND
ROMANCE

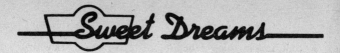

WEEKEND ROMANCE

Peggy Teeters

BANTAM BOOKS
NEW YORK • TORONTO • LONDON • SYDNEY • AUCKLAND

WEEKEND ROMANCE
A BANTAM BOOK 0 553 29988 3

First publication in Great Britain

PRINTING HISTORY
Bantam edition published 1995

Cover photo by Kim Hanson.

Bantam Books are published by Transworld Publishers Ltd,
61–63 Uxbridge Road, Ealing, London W5 5SA,
in Australia by Transworld Publishers (Australia) Pty Ltd,
15–25 Helles Avenue, Moorebank, NSW 2170,
and in New Zealand by Transworld Publishers (NZ) Ltd,
3 William Pickering Drive, Albany, Auckland.

Printed and bound in Great Britain by
Cox & Wyman Ltd, Reading, Berkshire.

Chapter One

On a Friday afternoon in early September, Katie Jean O'Connor dashed up the front steps of her house with her arms full of books and her head full of dreams—and tripped. The books flew in all directions as she suddenly found herself sprawled across the cement porch. Glancing furtively around to see if anyone had noticed, Katie was relieved to find nobody in sight. She rubbed her bruised knees, gathered up her belongings, and quickly slipped inside.

As she entered the cool, air-conditioned hallway, Katie shook her head in mock despair. She really had to stop daydreaming

about Scott McAllister! He was on her mind all the time. They had been dating off and on for months, and just last Saturday night under a starry sky Scott had asked her to go steady.

Katie knew she would never forget that wonderful moment. They had been to a dance at Shadow Lake, and as they were walking to Scott's car, he suddenly stopped, took Katie in his arms, and asked the question she'd been dying to hear. Naturally, Katie murmured that she would love to, and they sealed the bargain with a long, sweet kiss.

She could still hardly believe it! Scott McAllister was handsome, bright, and the best goalie on any soccer field. Why he had singled her out from all the gorgeous girls at Hillwood High was a mystery to Katie. Catching a glimpse of her reflection in the mirror over the hall table, she decided that since she certainly wasn't beautiful, Scott must like her turned-up nose and freckles.

"Katie, is that you?" her mother called from the kitchen. "I'm in here fixing potato salad to go with the fried chicken I made this morning. It's so hot today that I decided on a summer menu for dinner."

"It's me—or what's left of me," Katie said, dropping her books on the hall table. "You should have seen me a few minutes ago! Your daughter the klutz did an unexpected acrobatic number on the front steps and tripped over thin air. How many other people can beat that?"

"Are you all right?" Mrs. O'Connor, a small, attractive brunette, looked worried as Katie hobbled into the kitchen.

Katie grinned. "Oh, sure. Other than two sore knees, I'm perfectly okay. Watch—I'll show you." Grabbing the newspaper from the kitchen table, she rolled it into a tube and used it like a megaphone, chanting, "Yea, blue! Yea, white! Yea, Trojans! Fight, fight, *fight*!"

After the last "fight," Katie leaped into the air with such a whoop that Mrs. O'Connor clapped her hands over her ears.

"Okay, okay," her mother said, laughing. "You've convinced me! I can see that your lungs are in good shape, too—no wonder you made varsity cheerleader last year!" Shaking her head, she added, "I'll never understand how you manage to have so much energy after walking home from school in this hot

3

Georgia sun. I've spent most of the day slaving at my computer in the nice, cool den, and I'm beat."

"How's the book coming?" Katie asked. "Almost done?"

"Just two more chapters to go," her mother replied, briskly chopping a celery stalk. "Detective Russo is about to reveal the identity of the murderer in a staggering climax."

Katie perched on a stool by the kitchen counter. "Sounds cool," she said. "When are you going to put me in one of your mystery novels, Mom? Picture this—a sixteen-year-old, brown-haired beauty with super intelligence, overflowing with charm and charisma, a femme fatale who loves 'em and leaves 'em—"

"That's enough blarney for one day," her mother interrupted, laughing. "Do me a favor, honey. Run over to the PX and get me some new cards, will you? The Johnsons are coming over tonight for bridge and I don't dare bring out the ones we have. Willie keeps using them for his magic tricks, and they're really disgusting."

"Where is he, anyway?" Katie asked, picking up a piece of celery and popping it into her mouth.

"On a Cub Scout hike, with Mrs. Jennings in charge. She really should be given a medal for all she does for those kids."

Katie nodded. "I know what you mean. Any word from Danny? I really miss having my big brother around."

"Just a note," Mrs. O'Connor replied. "His classes have started, and he can already see that he'll have to hit the books every night without fail. Oh, and I got a nice letter from Judy telling me all about her dorm and her roommate. I'm so glad she decided to go to Duke instead of one of those New York colleges. Judy's a wonderful girl, but to tell you the truth, I was worried that she and Danny were getting a little too serious about each other. I think the distance between them will be good for them."

Carrying on the O'Connors' military tradition, Danny had been accepted at West Point and had left early in July for six weeks of intensive training known as "Beast Barracks." Katie was dying to visit him, and hoped her brother might even get her a blind date for a weekend at the Point.

5

Ever since she could remember, Katie had dreamed of strolling along Flirtation Walk with a handsome cadet and stopping in front of Kissing Rock. According to her mother, when that happened, the cadet would tell his date very seriously that if she didn't kiss him right away, the huge boulder would come tumbling down, crushing them both. His date, of course, would oblige, saving them from a horrible death.

Katie still looked forward to visiting West Point some day, but she was no longer interested in the kissing part. She was in love with a wonderful guy, and though Scott wasn't the least bit interested in a military career, Katie was sure no cadet, no matter how handsome he looked in his uniform, could possibly compare with Scott.

"Here are the car keys and some money," Mrs. O'Connor said. "My car is parked in the driveway."

Katie took the keys and stuffed the money into the pocket of her jeans. "Be back in a flash," she said, heading for the door. "I want to wash my hair before supper. Scott's taking me to see 'Cleopatra' at that little theater off-post—they show oldies but goodies

6

every Friday night. Later, we're going to the bon voyage party Carol's throwing for Debbie Clark. Her father's been assigned to Hawaii."

She left the house and hopped into her mother's old Mustang. As Katie drove down the street, she remembered her mother's concern about Danny and Judy getting too serious. *What if she knew how I feel about Scott?* she thought, but she knew exactly what her mother would say: "Oh, Katie, you're much too young!"

Katie had been hearing that from both her parents for years. When her father was stationed in Tokyo, Katie had started first grade at the age of five, as was customary for the children of American military families. Now, though she was only sixteen, she was entering her senior year of high school. All Katie's classmates were at least a year older than she, and her parents still thought of her as a little kid.

When Katie walked into the post exchange the woman at the door asked to see her ID card. Katie rummaged through her purse, searching for her wallet, but to her dismay it wasn't there. Though the clerk had seen her dozens of times, she said in an icy drone,

"Sorry. Regulations state that nothing can be purchased here without the proper ID. Next, please."

Blushing furiously with embarrassment, Katie stalked away, hoping she appeared cool and calm in spite of the fact that she was seething inside.

"Aha! Trying to sneak into a military installation without proper identification, huh?" someone whispered behind her.

Katie spun around and found a cute redhead standing there with a broad grin on her face. Laughing, she said, "Kelly, you rat! I'll get you for that! Gosh, I haven't seen you all day. Where have you been?"

"Packing, of course," Kelly Turner said. "You know that we leave at the crack of dawn tomorrow. Dad's job at the Pentagon begins next week." Her grin faded. "I really hate leaving all you guys and missing out on my senior year at Hillwood High."

Katie felt a lump form in her throat. She and Kelly had been friends for three years. They lived on the same street in Fort Benning, played soccer together, and had even fallen in love with the same boy two summers ago. Last year, they had decided on impulse to join the Thespians, the school drama club, and were amazed when they actually landed some good roles. Apparently they could act!

"Hey, come over here for a second," Katie said softly, taking Kelly aside. She explained her problem and asked Kelly to buy the deck of cards for her so she wouldn't have to make another trip. Kelly told her to wait outside, and a few minutes later, she joined Katie, handing her a package with a conspiratorial wink.

"Mission accomplished," she announced.

"Thanks, Kelly. You're a pal," Katie said.

Then the two of them stood there looking at each other, both suddenly at a loss for words. Katie knew it was time to say goodbye, and she also knew that it was possible they wouldn't see each other for a long, long time—maybe never. That was the way it was when your father or mother made a career of the military, and though Katie had experienced these partings many times, they never got any easier. *Sometimes life just isn't fair,* she thought sadly.

Forcing a smile, she gave Kelly a big bear hug. "Write to me from the far north, okay?"

Kelly laughed. "Virginia's not exactly the far north!"

"It is when you live down here in Georgia," Katie said. "You *will* write, won't you?"

"I'll do better than that. I'll call you just as soon as we get settled in our new house," Kelly promised. "In fact, I'll call you so often you'll hardly know I'm gone. My folks won't mind—they seem to like you, for some insane reason."

Katie made a face. "Thanks a lot! Well, take care, Red—take care . . ."

After one more quick hug, she walked quickly over to her car, trying to keep the tears from flowing.

When Katie arrived home and gave her mother the cards, Mrs. O'Connor told her there was a letter for her on the hall table. "You were so busy with your acrobatics that I guess you didn't see it when you came home this afternoon," she said, "and I forgot to mention it. It's from Paris."

Katie blinked in surprise. "Paris? You've got to be kidding! I don't know anybody there."

She hurried into the hall and scooped up

the books she'd dropped on the table earlier, setting them down on a nearby chair. Sure enough, there was a pink envelope addressed to her.

Katie picked up the envelope, looking for a return address, but there wasn't any. Though the handwriting looked vaguely familiar, for the life of her Katie couldn't recognize it. She tore open the envelope and took out the letter. As she read the short note, a big grin lit up her face.

"Mom! Mom!" she shouted, running back into the kitchen. "Guess what? Melissa Harris is coming to Fort Benning next week! General Harris is going to be stationed here. We were in Japan together when I was little, remember? I haven't seen her since we were all in Berlin four years ago. This is going to be so great!"

"Melissa Harris," her mother said thoughtfully. "Oh, yes, I remember her now. You two used to be good friends. But you don't hear from her very often anymore, do you? How come?"

"Well, her parents went through a kind of messy divorce," Katie told her. "Now Melissa

11

lives with her father most of the time. Her mother married a movie producer and moved to Hollywood."

"Really?" Mrs. O'Connor raised her eyebrows. "How glamorous!"

"We're still good friends even though we hardly ever write to each other." Katie smiled. "We like so many of the same things that it's unbelievable! We even *don't* like the same things—I'll never forget when Melissa and I were in first grade in Tokyo and we discovered that we both hated carrots. I knew right then that we were going to be friends forever! Wow, I can hardly wait to see Melissa again. I wonder if she's changed . . ."

She wandered out of the kitchen, reading the note a second time. Melissa couldn't have chosen a better time to return to the States. *It's not as if Melissa could take Kelly's place*, Katie thought. *But having her around will make losing Kelly a lot easier!*

Chapter Two

At dinner that night, Katie hoped that everyone would eat fast for once instead of dawdling over each course while they reported on the day's activities. But no such luck.

"Maggie, you'll never guess what I'll be having for supper when I fly down to Ranger Camp on Monday," Colonel O'Connor said to his wife.

Mrs. O'Connor winced. "I'm not sure I want to hear it," she replied, but he told her anyway.

"Sergeant Wilson is going to make me his specialty—roast alligator and rattlesnake!"

"Yuck! Gross!" Willie groaned.

Everybody laughed. They all knew that Willie even turned green at the sight of the chicken livers Mrs. O'Connor sometimes served for Sunday brunch.

"I guess Danny will have to eat that stuff, too," Willie said with a frown on his freckled face.

Katie was sure he had just made up his mind not to go into the military. She was equally sure he would change his mind by the next day, or even in the next five minutes. Willie idolized his father and brother, and in his eyes they could do no wrong.

Looking at him now, Katie noted as she had many times before how much Willie resembled their father. They both had blue eyes, freckles, and red hair, although Colonel O'Connor's was liberally sprinkled with gray. Willie would grow up to be just as good-looking as their father. *But I wish Dad would smile more often,* she thought. *He would be much more handsome.*

Katie knew how much Colonel O'Connor worried about the men in the Ranger program. Every cadet who went into the infantry after graduating from West Point had to take nine weeks of grueling training so he could become tough in mind and body, able to survive in any kind of terrain, from mountains to jungles. Three of those weeks were spent at Fort Benning, three at a camp in the mountains of northern Georgia, and the last three in the swamps of northwestern Florida. Colonel O'Connor was in charge of the Rangers, and felt responsible for each man.

Katie had asked him once what was the toughest challenge for him when he went through the training himself years ago. He'd said, "Walking through the swamps in water up to my neck and not knowing what else was in there with me!" Katie was sure she would faint if she ever had to do anything like that!

"Well, at least Danny made it through Beast Barracks," she said, reaching for a roll. "He said the King of the Beasts this year was a real monster. Even the upperclassmen steered clear of him."

"Oh, the plebes always exaggerate a bit, but somehow they manage to make it through those six weeks," her father said. "I have to admit, however, that when I was a plebe, there were times I was tempted to quit and study law instead."

Mrs. O'Connor raised her eyebrows. "Really? Somehow I can't picture you as a lawyer."

"Me neither," Willie agreed.

"Willie, how was your Cub Scout outing this afternoon?" his father asked.

Willie beamed. "Great, Dad! We learned why leaves change color in the fall, and Mrs. Jennings told us that some trees can signal to each other when they're in danger."

"Willie!" his mother exclaimed. "You're making that up!"

"No he isn't, Mom," Katie said. "I've heard the same thing." Changing the subject, she added, "Dad, I heard from Melissa Harris today. She and her father are coming to Benning very soon. Did you know that?"

"I heard about it two weeks ago, but I'm afraid it slipped my mind. You girls were good friends in Berlin, right?" Before Katie could reply, he continued, "Katie, are you going out tonight?"

"Yes—Scott and I are going to the early movie down at the Carrolton in Columbus, and then to a bon voyage party Carol Davis is giving for Debbie Clark," Katie told him.

Her father frowned. "Won't that get you home rather late?"

"Oh, no, Dad. We'll watch the time," Katie said in a very matter-of-fact tone. Whenever she spoke to her father about Scott, she was always extra careful not to give any indication of how much she cared for him. If Colonel O'Connor knew how she felt, he might not allow her to see Scott so often.

Sometimes it seemed to Katie that her father was living in the Dark Ages. A few months ago, she had asked her mother why he was so strict with her. Mrs. O'Connor had told her that his kid sister had run off with a boy and married him when she was Katie's age. She had a miserable life and died in childbirth at seventeen.

Katie hadn't known that, and she was sorry. But surely her father realized that she wouldn't do anything like that, no matter how crazy she was about Scott. Didn't he know that she was a responsible person with a good head on her shoulders? Didn't he know anything about her at all?

17

"Katie," her mother said now, "Willie and I can clear the table tonight. Why don't you go get ready for your date?"

"Thanks, Mom!" Katie jumped up from the table and rushed upstairs so she could use her jasmine bubble bath in peace without someone pounding on the door. Though there were three other bathrooms in the house, the big one at the top of the stairs seemed to be everybody's favorite.

After a long, luxurious soak, Katie slipped into a mint green sleeveless dress and tied a matching scarf around her long brown hair. Then she put on some raspberry lip gloss and dabbed a few drops of perfume behind each ear. She was standing in front of her dressing table checking her reflection in the mirror when she heard the grandfather clock in the hall strike seven times. Scott would be arriving any minute now.

As Katie went downstairs, she felt on top of the world. For the first time in her life, she loved a boy who loved her in return. And not just *any* boy, but a very special boy. Sometimes it seemed too good to be true!

Colonel O'Connor and Willie were out back playing catch and Katie's mother was in the kitchen when she let Scott in. He took one look at her and whistled. "Wow! You look fantastic," he said, smiling.

Katie stood on tiptoe to give him a quick kiss. "You say the sweetest things," she whispered.

Scott's expression as he looked at her made her heart pound so hard that Katie was sure it could be heard all through the house.

"Bye, Mom," she called. "I'll be home around twelve or so."

"Bye, dear. Have a wonderful time," her mother called back from the kitchen. "We'll leave the light on for you."

Katie smiled as she and Scott left the house hand in hand. Her mother said the same thing every time she went out on a date. Danny had heard those words when he was living at home, too, and Katie was sure that Willie would be hearing them in a few years.

As they drove downtown in Scott's Camaro, Katie kept stealing glances at him, thinking how his deep tan accented his blond good looks and his deep blue eyes. Yes, Scott was handsome all right, but what really endeared him to Katie was the way he treated her. He let her know in so many little ways that she was very important to him, and he often told her he loved her. Katie knew there weren't many boys who said that to their girlfriends even when they were going steady.

"Guess what?" Katie said, breaking the comfortable silence.

"It could be anything, coming from you," Scott teased.

Katie laughed. "Is that so? Well, it so happens that I have some *very* interesting news." She paused dramatically.

"I'm all ears."

"A friend of mine, a really terrific friend, is moving here in a few days!" Katie announced. "I can't wait for you to meet her. Her name's Melissa Harris, and she and her dad have been in Paris for the past two years. He's a general, and he's just been assigned to Fort Benning."

"What's this terrific friend of yours like?" Scott asked.

"I haven't seen Melissa in four years, but when we were in Berlin, she was blond and cute and funny and bubbly," Katie told him.

She decided not to mention the fact that at the time Melissa also had braces on her teeth, wore glasses, and was just a tad over-weight. "I thought maybe we could set her up with your friend Rick and the four of us could double some time. I bet they'd like each other."

"Sounds cool. Rick's not seeing anybody right now," Scott said. "He'd probably like to meet a new girl. I'll tell him about your friend."

"Great!" Katie said happily. "Now that's settled, I want you to tell me more about the time you went to the Valley of the Kings when your dad was stationed in Cairo a few years ago, and about Tutankhamen, the boy king. It'll get me in the right mood to see 'Cleopatra.' "

Scott laughed. "I must have told you all that a hundred times, but if you insist . . ."

He began describing the young king's tomb with all its treasures. Katie's favorite part of the story was the legend that the mummy of the young pharaoh had been found with a wreath of withered flowers around his head, placed there by his grieving bride. It was so romantic, and so sad.

Katie was sure they must have loved each other very much.

A short while later, supplied with popcorn and sodas, she and Scott settled down in their usual seats in the balcony. The lights went out, and Katie rested her head on Scott's shoulder, prepared to be swept away by the passion and pageantry on the screen.

As the story of Cleopatra unfolded and the beautiful, tempestuous queen entranced first Caesar and then Mark Antony, Katie wondered which man Cleopatra really loved. Or did she love them both? Katie couldn't imagine how that could be possible. She simply couldn't picture herself falling in love with two men.

After the show, Katie floated out of the theater and into Scott's car with her head in the clouds and tears in her eyes. She felt as though she had gone back in time to ancient Egypt where Cleopatra had ruled, loved, and died so long ago.

"Hey, Cleo, come back to the twentieth century," Scott said, smiling at her. "And fasten your seatbelt, or this chariot isn't going anywhere."

Katie blinked and fumbled with the buckle

of the webbing strap. "Sorry—you ought to know by now that I do this every time I see a really super movie," she said sheepishly. "I'd love to see it again some day."

"Ready to go to Carol's party?" Scott asked.

"Sure. Oh, by the way, I bought a bracelet for Debbie and signed the card from both of us."

Scott gave her a grateful glance. "Thanks, Katie. You think of everything. I never seem to get around to doing things like that."

When they arrived at Carol's house, Katie rang the bell and Carol opened the door almost immediately.

"Hey, you two! It's about time you showed up. Where have you been?" said the slender, dark-haired girl. "Oh, that's right—I forgot you went to the movies first. So what does Cleopatra have that Carol Davis doesn't, I'd like to know?" Then she laughed. "Don't you dare answer that question! Come on in."

Katie and Scott followed their hostess through the hallway and down a flight of steps to the recreation room where kids were talking, eating, and dancing to soft rock music. The room had been transformed into the stateroom of an ocean liner, complete with portholes and a huge golden anchor. A big wicker basket brimming over with luscious-looking fruit stood on a table in one corner. Nearby, brightly wrapped gifts were piled high, waiting for Debbie to open them.

Impressed by the decorations, Katie said, "Hey, Carol, everything looks great!"

"How did you do all this?" Scott asked.

"With the help of the Thespians," Carol told him. "The props are from 'Sail Away,' the musical we did last spring. Katie was in it, remember? Of course, Debbie and her dad will be flying, not sailing to Hawaii, but I thought the bon voyage theme called for something nautical. It's a lot more glamorous than the cabin of an airplane!"

After chatting a few minutes more, Katie and Scott went their separate ways. Katie made her way through the crowd to her friend Johnnie Warden, who was selecting music from Carol's huge collection of CDs. When he saw her, he grinned.

"Hi, Katie. Long time no see. When are you coming down to the station to do another 'Teen Scene' show with me?"

"Teen Scene" was a Saturday radio program on WTLC that featured Johnnie as dee-jay playing rock, rap, and country music. Though he was kind of skinny and not very good-looking, Johnnie had a deep, mellow voice that was perfect for radio. Occasionally Katie did a brief spot covering the latest fads and fashions, the newest movies, and the hottest bands. Sometimes she also inter-viewed kids from Hillwood High.

"I wish I could," she said. "I love working with you, Johnnie, but I have soccer practice almost every Saturday morning now."

"If you're serious, we could tape a show after school one day," Johnnie offered.

"Really? That would be super!" Katie said enthusiastically. "Just let me know the date about a week in advance so I can get my act together, okay?"

He nodded. "You're on!"

She was about to ask Johnnie some ques-tions about the show when Scott suddenly appeared at her side. "Sorry, Johnnie, but this girl belongs to me," he said with an en-gaging grin. "Come on, Katie—let's dance."

Taking Katie by the hand, he led her to the center of the floor where they joined many other couples dancing to a pulsing rock-and-roll beat. Soon, however, the music changed to a medley of dreamy, romantic tunes, and Katie closed her eyes as she and Scott swayed in each other's arms.

Later in the evening, Debbie opened her presents and exclaimed over every one of them. Katie could tell she was fighting back tears as she said, "I hope you'll all come to see me in Hawaii!"

When the party began to break up, Katie looked at her watch and saw that it was almost half past eleven. She also realized that she was starving—she hadn't eaten much supper and she'd hardly touched the snacks Carol had provided.

"Scott, let's stop at Joe's Place for a burger," she suggested as they got into the car.

"You just ate!" he said, laughing.

"No I didn't. I nibbled a little, that's all, and I'm dying for a Joe-burger and some fries."

"Well, okay," Scott said. "But I don't want your father to be mad at me if I don't get you home by twelve, Cinderella. You know how he is."

Katie sighed. "I sure do. But we'll make

the curfew. Joe's is only a few minutes from here."

Joe's Place was overflowing with hungry teenagers, however, and it was close to twelve-thirty when they pulled up in front of Katie's house. Scott walked her to the front door and put his arms around her. Snuggling close to him, Katie could hear his heart pounding as rapidly as her own. They kissed then, and Scott whispered, "I'm crazy about you, Katie, you know that?"

"Not half as crazy as I am about you," she murmured. "I'd better go in now. Call me tomorrow, okay? Maybe we can do something together on Saturday night."

Katie quietly opened the door, hoping that her father hadn't waited up for her.

Unfortunately, he had. Frowning, he said, "I thought you said you wouldn't be late."

"Sorry, Dad. We stopped at Joe's for a hamburger after the party and it was mobbed. I've never seen the place so crowded," Katie said nervously. "It wasn't Scott's fault—going to Joe's was my idea."

Colonel O'Connor shook his head wearily. "Katie, you're spending too much time with that boy, and I'm afraid you're getting too deeply involved." Before she could protest, he went on, "It's time we had a serious talk. But not tonight," he added, rubbing his eyes. "I'm tired, and I imagine you are, too. We'll have that talk first thing in the morning."

Her father turned and started up the stairs, leaving Katie standing in the hallway. Just a few minutes ago, she had been so happy, but now she felt both angry and worried. What would he say to her tomorrow? Would he forbid her to see Scott? And if he did, would she be able to persuade him to change his mind?

Chapter Three

But when Katie came down to breakfast the following day, she learned that her father had left for Ranger Camp early that morning. Relieved that the talk she'd been dreading had been postponed, she said to her mother, "I thought Dad wasn't going until Monday."

"One of the trainees almost drowned," Mrs. O'Connor said, a worried expression on her face. "The sergeant phoned at six this morning. He thinks there may be a problem with the new boats they've started using, and he asked your father to fly down right away."

"That's terrible!" Katie cried.

She and her mother sat at the kitchen table in silence for a moment. Then, "Let's change the subject, shall we?" Mrs. O'Connor suggested, forcing a smile. "Do you have soccer practice this morning, dear?"

Katie nodded. "Yes, and it's going to be a rough one. We're going to scrimmage a freshman team from Haviland, a girls' junior college outside of Atlanta—Coach Miller thought it would be a real challenge for the Blue Devils. Sara's picking me up in a few minutes. You know her—she's the tall, dark-haired girl who plays forward."

"Will you be playing halfback?" her mother asked.

"I hope so," Katie said. "Every now and then I have to play goalie, which I'm not nearly as good at. But, Mom, you really should see Scott play goalie. He's fantastic."

Just then a car horn honked outside, and Katie leaped to her feet. "That's Sara—gotta go. If Scott calls, please tell him I'll be back in the early afternoon, okay? I forgot to tell him about practice. Wish us luck—we'll need it!" she called as she dashed out the back door.

30

While the two girls drove to Atlanta, they discussed the game ahead of them.

"Do you think we can beat Haviland?" Katie asked.

"Of course we can," Sara said. "The Blue Devils are the best! I even heard a rumor that our team may be going to play in Europe next summer."

Katie was impressed. "Really? How about that! Scott's team is going to London during spring break to be in a special tournament. They've been having yard sales and washing cars to raise money for their expenses. We could do the same thing."

"Speaking of Scott, how's the great love of your life?" Sara asked, glancing over at her.

Smiling, Katie said, "Couldn't be better. We see each other almost every day. It's getting so I'm beginning to think I can't live without him!" She blushed. "Sounds melodramatic, doesn't it, like something from a soap opera? You know, until Scott and I started going out, I didn't think I'd ever get serious about a guy. Boy, was I wrong! I'm in love, *really* in love."

"Well, good luck," Sara said dryly. "I felt

31

the same way last summer when my family stayed at our beach house. I met this boy, and we were together every minute. I was so crazy about Kevin . . ." Her voice trailed off.

"So what happened?" Katie asked.

Sara shrugged. "Nothing. I never saw him again after vacation, and now I hardly remember what he looks like."

"I'll never forget Scott," Katie said softly. "Never, ever!"

"How about trying to forget about him just until after the scrimmage?" Sara joked. "If you're drifting around somewhere on Cloud Nine, we don't stand a chance of beating those JC girls!"

As it happened, the Blue Devils won by a score of 2 to 1, rallying on a rebound in the last few minutes. Katie was eager to tell Scott all about it when he called later that afternoon, but he had some news of his own.

"Listen, Katie, I'm afraid I can't see you tonight," he said. "Something's come up, a family emergency. My grandmother had a heart attack and we're flying to Chicago in about an hour. We probably won't get back until Tuesday or Wednesday."

"Oh, I'm so sorry!" Katie exclaimed. "I hope she'll be all right."

"Me too," Scott said. "By the way, did you get any flak about getting home late last night?"

"Well, Dad wasn't too thrilled," Katie admitted. "But don't worry about it, Scott. You have enough on your mind right now. I hope your grandmother gets better real fast. Call me the minute you get back, okay?"

"Will do. Love you, Katie."

"Love you too."

As Katie hung up the phone, she suddenly felt very lonely. She was missing Scott already, and he hadn't even left yet!

Since she had nothing else to do that evening, Katie found her mother's well-worn copy of *Gone with the Wind* and curled up with it in a comfortable chair in the den. Though she had read it before many years ago, she soon lost herself in Scarlett O'Hara's story, and was startled when her mother came into the room and turned on her computer.

"You're not going to work now, are you, Mom?" Katie asked.

"No, dear. I just want to see where I left off in my storyline this morning so I can plot the next chapter in my head," Mrs. O'Connor replied. "No date tonight?"

Katie shook her head. "Scott had to fly to Chicago with his family. His grandmother's very ill."

"What a shame! I hope she'll be all right." Glancing at Katie's book as she left the den, her mother said, "That's one of my favorite novels. Did you know that Margaret Mitchell originally named her heroine 'Pansy'? She changed it to Scarlett at the last minute."

"*Katie* Scarlett," Katie corrected, smiling. "Good thing she did. Pansy O'Hara sounds ridiculous!"

She returned to the novel, and became so swept up in the passions of Scarlett and Rhett that she almost didn't think about Scott. Almost, but not quite.

On Sunday, Katie called her friend Kimmie Martin to tell her that she had decided not to go bowling as they had planned because she just had to finish *Gone with the Wind.*

"I don't blame you," Kimmie said. "I've read it twice, and I saw the movie on TV the other night for about the seventh time. See you at lunch tomorrow, I guess."

Good old Kimmie, Katie thought as they hung up. Kimmie was one of her closest friends. They ate lunch together every day in the school cafeteria, talking about everything—the latest rumors going around Hillwood High, who was dating whom, and on Katie's part, how wonderful Scott McAllister was. Though Kimmie had never said anything specific, Katie got the impression that for some reason she didn't like Scott very much, but her friend always listened patiently and kept her comments to herself.

Late that night after finishing the book, Katie went to bed wondering what it would have been like to live on a plantation during the War Between the States. She pictured herself as Scarlett O'Hara and Scott as Rhett Butler, sweeping her off her feet and crushing her in his manly arms.

But as she turned off the light, Katie sighed. Now that she had emerged from the excitement of that long-ago world, she missed Scott more than ever. *Thank goodness he'll be home soon*, she thought just before she drifted off to sleep. *Maybe even the day after tomorrow!*

*   *   *

But to Katie's disappointment, Scott wasn't in school on Tuesday. That afternoon as she wandered aimlessly around the house, she heard a knock at the door. Hoping it might be Scott, Katie flew to open it.

It wasn't Scott. Instead, a stunning blonde stood there with a dazzling smile on her tanned face. When Katie just stared at her in confusion, the girl said, "For Pete's sake, Katie, aren't you going to ask me in? It's me—Melissa!"

Katie could hardly believe her eyes. Gone were the glasses, the braces, the extra pounds. This girl was drop-dead gorgeous— tall, willowy, and elegantly dressed in a teal blue washed silk shirt and a short white skirt that showed off her long, slender legs. It *couldn't* be Melissa, but apparently it was.

Letting out a squeal of delight, Katie threw her arms around her long-lost friend. "Melissa!" she cried as the two girls embraced. "It really *is* you!"

Laughing, Melissa said, "Who did you think it was, silly? The Avon lady?"

Katie took her by the hand and pulled her

inside. "I just don't believe this!" she exclaimed. "You look fabulous!"

"Thanks. You look pretty good yourself," Melissa said with a smile.

"Come on into the kitchen—we have to celebrate!" Katie led the way, then pointed to a stool next to the counter. "Now you sit right there while I raid the refrigerator. And don't you *dare* tell me you're on a diet."

"Not anymore." Melissa perched on the stool.

Katie quickly found some cheese, the rest of the guacamole her mother had made the night before, and two cans of soda. Putting everything on the counter along with a box of crackers and a bag of tortilla chips, she sat down next to Melissa.

"This is just like old times," she said happily. "Remember how we used to pig out in Berlin before we went out searching for spies?"

Melissa giggled. "How could I forget? We were at the American School—you were twelve and I'd just turned thirteen. We followed that weird-looking man down the street, and we were so sure he was a spy that we even trailed him into that spooky old house!"

"And then we accidentally locked ourselves in the attic," Katie recalled. "Your father had to send some soldiers to look for us, and we were both grounded for three whole weeks!

"Okay, enough about the past. Now I want to know how you turned into this gorgeous creature," Katie said, munching on a tortilla chip. "A fairy godmother granted you three wishes and this was one of them, right?"

Melissa made a face. "Believe me, Katie, it wasn't that easy. This ugly duckling became a swan because she spent the summers in Hollywood with her beautiful mother who couldn't stand the sight of her, so she made some changes."

She sounded so bitter that Katie was shocked. "That's not true—is it?"

Smiling slightly, Melissa said, "Would I lie to you? Yes, it's true. Now Mom's pleased with the results and I have to admit I am too, but it was pretty awful there for a while. I mean, I never dreamed my parents would get a divorce and I'd spend my time shuttling between Mom and Dad." She sighed. "There are times when I still can't believe it. I'm finally starting to make friends with Harry, Mom's new husband, but it's taking forever."

At that point, Mrs. O'Connor came into the kitchen loaded down with groceries. Her reaction when she saw Melissa was exactly what Katie's had been, and after Katie explained who Melissa was, she shook her head in amazement. "*This* is the girl who told me four years ago that she didn't care what she looked like because she was going to dedicate her life to science?"

Grinning, Melissa said, "You have to realize that at the time I was madly in love with my biology teacher. Mr. Hadley was a real dreamboat, remember, Katie?"

"Not really. I was too busy falling in love with my English teacher and learning to write sonnets," Katie replied.

"You girls!" Mrs. O'Connor laughed as she and Katie began to put the groceries away. "We're so glad you're here, Melissa. As soon as you're settled in your new place, I want you and your father to come to dinner and tell us everything that's been happening to you."

"I'd like that and I'm sure Dad would too,"

Melissa said. "But right now I'd better get back to the house. The movers are there unpacking and I want to make sure that they put our things into the right rooms." She stood up and dusted a few cracker crumbs from her white skirt. "Katie, call me tonight and fill me in about school, okay? I don't know anything about Hillwood High."

Katie tore off a piece of paper from the notepad next to the phone, and Melissa wrote down her phone number and address.

"Mom's letting me use the car for the rest of the week while Dad's in Florida," Katie said as she walked her friend to the front door. "Why don't I pick you up at seven-thirty?"

"How do you get to school when you don't drive?" Melissa asked.

"By bus. Lots of the kids on post do that."

Wrinkling her nose, Melissa said, "Sounds tacky. Listen, when I know my way around, I'll pick *you* up in my new red Porsche."

"Your *what*?" Katie squawked.

"My Porsche," Melissa repeated, indicating the gleaming scarlet sports car parked at the curb. "It's a real early Christmas present from Harry, my filthy rich stepfather. Talk to you later!"

Katie stared after her as Melissa walked briskly to the car, got in, and drove away, her long golden hair streaming behind her.

"Wow," she whispered. "Wait till the kids at school get a load of that!"

Chapter Four

That night around nine o'clock, Scott finally phoned. "Hi there," he said. "I'm back. Grandma's doing much better, or at least that's what the doctors say. As far as I can tell, she really is. She's talking about playing bridge, and she can't wait to start going to all her club meetings again."

"I'm so glad," Katie said. "Guess what, Scott? My friend Melissa, the one I told you about, just arrived today. I'll introduce you to her at school tomorrow." She paused, then added mischievously, "Oh, and by the way, I have a confession to make. I fell madly in love while you were gone."

"You did *what*?" Scott sounded horrified.

Laughing, Katie said, "I fell in love with Rhett Butler all over again! I've been reading *Gone with the Wind* ever since you left to keep myself from missing you so much."

Scott let out an exaggerated sigh of relief. "Whew! You had me going there for a minute. I thought maybe you'd really started dating some other guy."

"You know I'd never do that. You're the only one for me," Katie assured him tenderly. "And anyway, it didn't really work. I missed you like crazy, and I can't wait to see you tomorrow."

"Me either," Scott said. "Love you, Katie."

"Love you too, Scott," she said. "With all my heart."

On Wednesday morning Katie picked up Melissa, who looked lovely in an oversized pale blue cotton sweater and designer jeans. Katie was wearing an oversized pale green sweater and designer jeans, and the minute they saw each other, the girls burst out laughing.

"Still hate carrots?" Katie asked as she drove down the tree-lined street.

"Sure do!" Melissa giggled. "What about you?"

"Can't stand 'em!"

"So how's your love life, Katie?"

Startled by Melissa's abrupt change of subject, Katie said, "What made you ask that right now?"

Melissa shrugged. "I don't know. Just curious, I guess. Well, are you going to tell me or not?"

"Actually, it's pretty good," Katie said, smiling. "I'm dating a guy named Scott McAllister—you'll meet him today. He's a handsome hunk, and for some weird reason he seems to think I'm pretty special. What about you?"

"Oh, I was going with a French boy in Paris for a while, but I ditched him when I found out he was seeing somebody else on the side," Melissa told her.

"Bummer," Katie said sympathetically. "But don't worry—there are dozens of cute guys at Hillwood High, and as soon as they see you, I bet there'll be a stampede!"

When they arrived at school, Katie gave Melissa a whirlwind tour, then took her to the main office. Melissa had to present her transcript from her school in Paris, find out what subjects she'd have to take, and what her class schedule would be.

Before Katie left her there, she said, "My lunch period is eleven-thirty. If yours is the same, look for me in the cafeteria at the end table to the left next to the window—I'll be sitting with my friend Kimmie. If we miss each other, meet me in the hall in front of the trophy case at two-thirty, okay?"

"Yes, *ma'am*!" Melissa said, giving her a smart salute.

Katie grinned and headed for her first class, World Lit. As she walked quickly down the hall, she saw Scott coming toward her, and her heart leaped.

"Hi, stranger," she said, raising her face for his kiss.

"Hi yourself." Scott put his arm around her shoulders. "Listen, Katie, I just found out that Stevenson sprung a test in World Lit yesterday, and I'll have to take a makeup tomorrow. Think you could update me on the garbage I missed while I was away?"

"Excuse me, but Shakespeare's sonnets are *not* garbage," Katie huffed.

He gave her one of those incredible smiles

45

that always turned her to jelly. "Just kidding. It's just that you're so good at stuff like that and I'm so hopeless. Will you help me? Please?"

"Sure," Katie said. "How about right after school?"

Scott shook his head. "Can't—soccer practice. Why don't you call me tonight and give me all the details?"

Katie promised she would, and they went into the classroom together.

For the next fifty-five minutes, she tried to concentrate while her favorite teacher talked about her favorite subject, but her mind kept wandering to Melissa. She hoped her friend wasn't feeling lonely or finding her first day at Hillwood too confusing.

Katie looked forward to seeing Melissa at lunch, but though she scanned the crowd in the cafeteria while she and Kimmie ate, she didn't see Melissa anywhere. She finally found her in the main hall at the end of the school day. Melissa was surrounded by a group of admiring kids, chiefly boys. One of them was Scott. As soon as he saw Katie, he came over to her, a stunned expression on his face.

"You said Melissa was a cute, bubbly little blonde," he said. "I sure wasn't expecting somebody who looks like a movie star!"

Laughing, Katie said, "Believe me, she's changed a lot. I didn't even recognize her when she came to the house yesterday." Then she added mischievously, "Now that you've seen her, do you think Rick might possibly be interested in taking her out?"

"Not possibly—*definitely*," Scott replied with a grin. "When we talk tonight, let's set something up." He gave her a quick peck on the cheek. "Gotta run, or I'll be late for soccer practice."

After he left, Katie hung around on the fringes of the crowd, wondering how long she would have to wait for Melissa. At last Melissa caught sight of her and waved. "You don't have to give me a lift, Katie," she sang out. "This nice boy has just offered to drive me home. Right, Ralph?"

"Ron," the curly-haired boy next to her corrected.

"Sorry—Ron." Melissa fluttered her long lashes, and the goofy grin on Ron's face broadened. "Call you tonight, Katie!"

As Katie headed for the exit, she smiled to

47

herself. *And I was worried about Melissa being lonely!* she thought. It was obvious that loneliness was not going to be a problem. Melissa was having no trouble making new friends, no trouble at all!

That Friday evening, Katie and Scott double-dated with Rick and Melissa. They had agreed that the boys would pick up the girls at Katie's house, then go to a movie.

"Good! We're not doing our Bobbsey Twins routine tonight," Melissa said when she arrived. She was wearing black jeans, a white tunic top, and a purple linen blazer, while Katie had on a denim miniskirt and an outsized navy-and-red-striped jersey. "Now quick, before the guys get here, tell me something about Rick," Melissa went on. "He must be the only guy at Hillwood High that I haven't met."

"Okay, here goes," Katie said. "Rick's a friend of Scott's—but you already know that. He's tall, with sandy-colored hair and brown eyes and a really nice smile, he's a dynamite tennis player . . ." She glanced out the window. "And here he comes now!"

"He sounds cool," Melissa said, following

Katie to the door. "I simply *adore* tennis players!"

The minute Rick saw Melissa, it was apparent that he was bowled over. Taking her hand, he gazed into her eyes and said, "I've heard a lot about you, Melissa, but nothing I've heard does you justice."

"Why, thank you, kind sir," Melissa murmured. "I thought only French boys knew how to pay a girl a compliment, but I guess I was wrong."

On the short drive to the movie theater, Melissa and Rick sat in the backseat, and Melissa devoted her entire attention to Rick.

"Katie tells me you play a mean game of tennis," she cooed. "Are you thinking of turning pro? It's such a glamorous, exciting career!"

"Well, that's a possibility," Rick replied, "but lately I've been thinking of studying medicine instead."

"You're kidding!" Scott exclaimed.

"Since when?" Katie asked.

"I guess since my last visit to my grandfather. He's a country doctor in southern Virginia, and he'd be very happy if I took over his practice some day."

"A country doctor?" asked Melissa, sounding dismayed. "They work awfully hard and they don't make much money, right?"

"True, but they do an awful lot of good," Rick said.

"I suppose so . . ." After a brief pause, Melissa said brightly, "So Katie, what movie are we seeing tonight? The new Kevin Costner flick?"

"No—'Gaslight,' with Ingrid Bergman and Charles Boyer," Katie told her. "It's a classic. I've seen it twice, and it's scary, suspenseful, and wonderful!"

They were soon seated in the theater, and when the lights went off and the film began, Katie snuggled close to Scott. She noticed that Melissa and Rick had their heads together, whispering to each other and looking very cozy. But she soon forgot about everything except the enthralling drama being played out on the screen.

For almost two hours, the movie held Katie spellbound. When it was over, she walked out of the theater in her customary daze, hardly aware of Scott and Rick's comments on the film. Melissa's voice brought her back to reality.

"It was all right, I guess," Melissa was saying, "but don't you think it was just a little bit corny?"

Katie stared at her in surprise. "I thought you loved old movies."

Shrugging, Melissa said, "I used to, but not anymore. I guess it's because I've spent so much time going to screenings in Hollywood lately that old movies look—well, *old*, if you know what I mean."

"In Hollywood? Really? Tell me about that," Rick said eagerly.

So Melissa did, all the way to Pete's Pizza Parlor. Both Rick and Scott hung on her every word, but though Katie was interested in what her friend had to say, she couldn't help wondering if the changes she'd been noticing in Melissa were more than skin deep.

Once they were seated in a booth at Pete's, however, Melissa was her old familiar self. She and Katie ordered the exact same thing—two slices with artichoke hearts and extra cheese—and the boys watched in amazement as they devoured every crumb including the crust.

On Saturday evening, the four of them went to a barbecue at Johnnie Warden's house. After Katie and Scott had mingled for a while and tasted some of the food, they walked to a secluded corner of the yard where they could be by themselves for a few minutes under the golden harvest moon.

"Those torch lights around the tables are much too bright," Scott grumbled.

"People have to be able to see what they're eating," Katie pointed out. "Everything's delicious, and I'm going back for more—later. Oh, Scott," she sighed, "just look at all those stars!"

"I'd rather look at my favorite cowgirl," Scott said, taking her in his arms. "You look so pretty in that white western outfit."

They kissed, and all the stars in the sky seemed to be dancing behind Katie's closed eyelids. *It just doesn't get any better than this*, she thought dreamily.

When they finally joined the others loading up their plates with more barbecue, beans, and salad, Melissa and Rick also helped themselves to seconds. Like Katie, Melissa was dressed western-style, but her outfit was all black, including her snakeskin boots and cowboy hat. Katie thought she looked amazing, and apparently Rick and most of the other boys did too. They buzzed around Melissa like flies around honey. Their dates weren't too happy about it, but Katie could tell that Melissa loved all the attention, laughing and flirting with each boy in turn.

Near the end of the evening, Katie lost sight of Scott. Wandering away from the gang to look for him, she saw him talking to Melissa in the shadows of a tall oak tree. As Katie started to walk over to them, she saw Melissa fling her arms around Scott's neck and kiss him right on the mouth.

Katie stopped in her tracks. What was going on?

Nothing, she told herself immediately. *Absolutely nothing. Melissa likes to flirt, that's all. And people kiss people all the time in France. It doesn't mean a thing. Don't be paranoid.* But her smile as she joined them was a little forced.

Katie managed to put the incident out of her mind until Scott pulled up in front of her house later that night after dropping off Rick and Melissa.

Rather than nestling into his arms for a

goodnight kiss, she said casually, "Uh . . . Scott, now that you've gotten to know Melissa, what do you think of her?"

"Really attractive, but kind of an airhead," he replied promptly. "Sorry, Katie—I know she's your childhood buddy, but you wanted my opinion and you got it." He kissed the tip of her nose. "Now let's talk about us. When are we going to get together *without* Rick and Melissa breathing down our necks?"

Relieved by Scott's brisk dismissal of her friend, Katie smiled and moved closer to him. "Well, maybe we can go out tomorrow evening for a little while, but I'll have to get back early so I can study for my physics test on Monday. If I work real hard, maybe I can get a decent grade for once. Physics is my *worst* subject."

"If you need any help, just let me know," Scott said. "It happens to be one of my best."

Katie sighed. "How come you don't have any trouble learning all that stuff? Better teacher?"

Grinning, Scott said, "Nope—better brain, love!"

"I'll get you for that!" Katie cried.

She dug her fingers into his ribs and

began tickling him. Scott retaliated until, weak with laughter, Katie begged for mercy. Then, after a long, thrilling kiss, they agreed that Scott would come by for her at seven o'clock Sunday evening, and he drove off.

I must have been crazy to worry about him and Melissa, Katie thought as she walked up the path to her house. *If I can't trust the boy I love with my oldest friend, I can't trust anybody at all!*

Chapter Five

Over the next two weeks, Katie saw very little of Melissa except at soccer practice. Despite her late entry to Hillwood High, Melissa, an excellent goalie, had made the team and impressed all the Blue Devils with her skill. But the two girls had no classes together, they didn't share the same lunch period, and after Johnnie's barbecue, Melissa and Rick never double-dated with Katie and Scott again. According to Scott, Rick had asked her out several times, but she always made some excuse, and Rick finally gave up.

One day in the locker room after soccer

practice, Katie decided to find out why Melissa had dropped Rick like a hot potato.

"How come you're not dating Rick anymore?" she asked.

"Oh, I don't know," Melissa said, combing her long blond hair in front of the mirror. "Rick's nice, but he's not very exciting, and he's awfully unsophisticated. Actually," she added, "I've started seeing the son of one of Dad's friends in Atlanta. His name's Grey Lockwood, and his family belongs to a really posh country club. I spent last weekend with him and his family."

Katie couldn't think of anything to say, but it made her sad that she and Melissa seemed to be drifting apart.

Katie wasn't seeing very much of Scott, either, except in World Lit. Even though they no longer had to worry about being part of a foursome when they went out, their dates had been few and far between ever since her dad returned from Florida. Also, when the girls' soccer team wasn't practicing after school, the boys' team was, and Scott's team played a lot of out-of-town games, which took up many of his weekends. Though Katie and Scott spoke on the phone almost every night, she couldn't help feeling lonely, both for him and for Melissa.

One Saturday evening when Katie was sitting at home watching TV with her family, Johnnie Warden called to ask if she'd like to tape a "Teen Scene" show on Monday afternoon. "How about an interview?" he suggested. "You haven't done one of those in a long time."

"Gee, Johnnie, I'd like to," Katie said, "but this is awfully short notice. I'm not sure I can find anybody . . ." And then she had a sudden inspiration. "Listen, Johnnie, what if I try to set up an interview with Melissa Harris? She's had a really interesting life and she's a good friend of mine." *Or at least she used to be,* Katie thought.

Johnnie loved her idea. "The blond bombshell? No doubt! Too bad the show's not on TV—our ratings would fly sky high!"

As soon as Katie hung up, she dialed the Harrises' number, hoping Melissa would be home on a Saturday night. To her surprise, Melissa herself answered the phone.

"Hey, it's Katie. What are *you* doing home tonight? Taking a break from your busy social calendar?"

"Well, the Lockwoods invited me for the

58

weekend again, but I'm getting bored with Grey so I didn't go. What's up?"

When Katie told her about the radio program, Melissa sounded delighted and eagerly agreed to be interviewed. After they discussed possible questions Katie might ask, they talked and giggled for almost an hour. By the time they hung up, Katie felt sure that their friendship was firmly back on track.

Monday's "Teen Scene" taping went off without a hitch. Johnnie assured Katie and Melissa that it would be a big hit with the show's listeners when it aired on Saturday afternoon.

Afterwards, Katie asked Melissa if she'd mind dropping her at the school athletic field so she could watch some of Scott's soccer practice. "You don't have to hang out or anything," she added as Melissa's flashy red Porsche pulled away from the curb. "Scott will drive me home."

Melissa grinned. "Believe me, it's no hardship watching a bunch of cute guys running around in shorts, and Scott's the cutest one of all. How long have you two been going together, anyway?"

"Well, we started seeing each other in May," Katie said, "but he only asked me to go steady about a month ago."

"You've been dating the same guy for *six months*?" Melissa sounded incredulous. "Ever since that Frenchman I told you about, I've made it a rule never to date anybody for more than a couple of weeks—at the most."

Katie smiled. "Then I guess you've never been in love."

"I guess not," Melissa agreed. "So you think you're in love with Scott?"

"I don't think, I *know*," Katie said firmly.

"Is he in love with you?"

"Of course he is. I mean, he says he is . . ." Katie frowned. "Is it so hard to believe that a guy like Scott could be in love with a girl like me?"

Melissa laughed. "Don't be silly! Maybe I'm just a little bit jealous, that's all." She slowed the car to a stop next to the athletic field. "Here we are. Enjoy your ride home with Prince Charming!"

Katie got out and gazed after the red Porsche as Melissa drove away. *She can't really be jealous of me, can she?* Katie wondered as she began making her way across the field to where the soccer team was practicing. *No, that's ridiculous. What have I got that Melissa doesn't have, except Scott?*

When soccer practice was over, Scott treated Katie to a sundae at The Igloo, their favorite ice cream parlor. It was the closest thing they'd had to a date in a long time, and they had a lot of catching up to do. After they compared notes on schoolwork and the progress of the girls' and boys' soccer teams, Katie eagerly told Scott all about her Teen Scene interview with Melissa.

"She was really great," Katie said. "Wait till you hear her stories about the Hollywood stars she's met! Her stepfather even got Melissa a bit part in one of his movies—no lines, but she's on screen for almost five minutes in a party scene. It'll air on Saturday morning," she added, then laughed. "The interview, I mean, not the movie!"

"Sounds cool, but I guess I'll have to miss it," Scott said. "We've got a game, as usual." He took a spoonful of his hot fudge sundae. "So what else is going on with your glamorous movie-star friend these days?"

"Well, Melissa was dating some guy in Atlanta," Katie told him, "but they just broke up."

"Figures," Scott said, frowning. "She probably ditched him the way she ditched Rick. I wonder what poor sap she'll hit on next?"

Katie frowned. "Scott, don't be mean! I admit that Melissa likes to play the field, but that doesn't make her a bad person. And she *is* my friend, remember."

"Just because she's your friend doesn't mean I have to like the way she acts," he said grumpily.

"Scott . . ." Katie warned.

Shrugging, he said, "Okay, okay, I'll shut up. If you're finished with that tutti-frutti thing, let's hit the road. I've got some major studying to do for tomorrow, and all of a sudden I'm not feeling too good. Maybe I shouldn't have eaten that sundae."

"Oh, Scott, I hope you're not coming down with something," Katie said. "There's a lot of stomach flu going around. Kimmie's been out of school with it since last Friday."

Scott smiled at her. "Don't worry about me—I never get sick. Like I said, it's probably just too much hot fudge."

As soon as he had paid for their ice cream, Scott took Katie home.

"See you tomorrow," he said just before she got out of the car, and gave her a quick kiss on the cheek. "Love you," he added as he always did.

"Love you, too," Katie replied as she always did. As Scott drove away, she realized with a sudden pang that they both spoke those words automatically, almost like saying "Bless you" when somebody sneezed.

But that's all right, Katie told herself, walking slowly up the path to her front door. *Just because we don't really think about what we're saying doesn't mean it isn't true. . . .*

She had just come into the house when Willie came racing up to her, all excited. "Guess what, Katie? Mom and Dad got a letter from Danny today, and so did I, and you did too!" he cried. "Yours is on the hall table. I wanted to open it for you, but Mom wouldn't let me."

Laughing, Katie picked up the envelope. "Good for Mom!"

"I'm going up to my room to answer my letter right away," Willie announced, and pounded up the stairs.

As she opened the letter, Katie felt guilty. It had been ages since she had written to Danny, and she was sure he'd remind her of that fact.

She was right. The letter read:

Dear Katie,

Remember me? I'm your brother Danny, the one at West Point. Mom and Dad are pretty good about writing, and I've even gotten a couple of scrawls from Willie, but I haven't heard from you in months. What gives??? It would be nice if you scribbled a note once in a while. We all look forward to mail up here, even if it's only from a kid sister. (Just kidding!)

Now here's my real reason for this letter. My roommate, Ben Anderson, saw a snapshot of you the other day and he thinks you're "mighty cute" (his words, not mine!). Ben's from Montana and he's a real good guy. He asked if maybe you'd like to come up to the Point for a weekend soon, and I told him I'd find out. If you'd be interested in a parade, a football game, and a personal guided

*tour of this citadel on the Hudson, let me
know right away and I'll pass the word
along. Ben will write to you with all the
details as soon as I hear from you.*

Love,
Danny

Katie read the letter over and over, her
thoughts churning. Here was the invitation
she'd been longing for ever since she was a
little girl! It was a dream come true—or it
would have been before she met Scott. Now
Katie didn't know what to do. Much as she
wanted to accept Danny's offer, how could
she possibly agree to a blind date at West
Point when she had a steady boyfriend here
at home?

Chapter Six

After a restless night, Katie was still in a quandary when she took the bus to school the next morning. She had to respond to Danny's invitation very soon, but she simply didn't know what to say.

Maybe I ought to talk to Scott about it, Katie thought as she headed for her World Literature class. *Yes, that's what I'll do. I'll explain the situation and ask him how he feels about it. And if he doesn't want me to go, I won't.*

But Scott wasn't there, and when class was over, Katie found Rick waiting for her in the hall. He told her that Scott had come down with the flu and might not be back in school for several days.

"He asked me to tell you not to worry, and that he'll give you a call once he feels a little better," Rick added. "He's feeling so lousy that he could hardly talk when I phoned him last night."

"Poor Scott." Katie sighed. "Thanks for delivering the message, Rick."

"No problem," Rick said, and they went their separate ways.

Though she was terribly sorry that Scott was sick, Katie couldn't help thinking that it might just be a blessing in disguise. It would give her an opportunity to think about how best to broach the subject the next time they spoke.

If only Kimmie wasn't sick too I'd ask her advice, Katie said to herself as she walked down the hall. *She's good at stuff like this.*

Absorbed in her own thoughts, Katie didn't notice the crowd of kids peering at the bulletin board near the guidance office until her friend Carol called, "Hey, Katie, take a look at this!"

"What's going on?" she asked, coming closer.

"The Thespians are doing 'Brigadoon,' " Johnnie Warden told her. "They're holding tryouts this Thursday and Friday."

"Oh, I love that show!" Katie exclaimed happily. "My Aunt Sheila's an actress, and she played the lead, Fiona, in the Broadway revival a few years ago. She was great—my whole family went up to New York to see it."

"So are you going to audition?" Johnnie asked.

"Gosh, I don't know," Katie said. "I'd love to try out for Fiona, and I guess I'd have the time once soccer season ends, but I don't think I have a good enough voice."

Melissa suddenly appeared at her side. "A good enough voice for what, Katie?"

When Katie explained about the auditions for "Brigadoon," Melissa raised one eyebrow. "I'm not crazy about amateur theatricals myself," she said, "although I did play a small role in a theater club production of 'Cabaret' when I was in Paris. But by all means go for it if you want to. In fact, I might try out too, just for fun."

"If you did, what part would you audition

for?" Johnnie asked, gazing adoringly at Melissa.

"Well, since Fiona's the lead, I'd definitely try for that," she said, and gave Katie a playful nudge. "Wouldn't it be cool if we were in competition for the same part? We haven't done that since we both tried out for Maria in the school production of 'The Sound of Music' when we were in Berlin! I got it, remember?"

Katie nodded, forcing a smile. "Yes, I do. I got the part of the Mother Superior at the convent."

"And you were wonderful," Melissa enthused. "You proved what Miss Mullins, our drama teacher, always said about there being no small parts, only small actors."

Tucking her arm through Katie's, she drew her away from the rest of the kids and murmured, "Listen, if you're not doing anything after school today, Katie, could you possibly give me some help with my trig homework? I'll drive you home, and we could study at your house. Unless you have a date with Scott, of course," she added.

"No—Scott has the flu," Katie told her. "I'll

meet you in the parking lot by your car, okay?"

Melissa gave Katie's arm a friendly squeeze. "Terrific! See you then!"

As Katie hurried to her next class, she had a brilliant idea. Melissa was her oldest friend in all the world. She would ask Melissa how she should approach Scott about Danny's invitation to a West Point weekend.

"All *right*!" Melissa exclaimed when Katie showed her Danny's letter later that afternoon. "This is so exciting I can hardly believe it! It's a dream date—you absolutely, positively have to go!"

When Katie didn't say anything, Melissa stared at her. "You *are* going, aren't you?"

"How can I, when I'm going steady with Scott?" Katie said. "Unless he says it's okay, of course. I'm going to tell him about it when I talk to him tomorrow, but I thought maybe you could give me some pointers about what to say so he doesn't take it the wrong way."

Melissa flopped back in her chair, stared up at the ceiling of Katie's bedroom, and groaned. "You have to be out of your mind, Katie Jean O'Connor! Scott will never agree

70

to your spending an entire weekend with some other guy, even if he is just your brother's roommate. He'll never understand that something like this isn't a real date—it's an *event*! You can't tell him about it, you just can't!"

"I have to," Katie insisted. "If I can't be honest with Scott, I won't go."

Melissa leaned forward. "Picture yourself walking down Flirtation Walk with a handsome cadet. Picture yourself watching a parade and a football game with him, and staying at the Thayer Hotel with starlets and models, as well as the other dates of the cadets. You might never get another invitation!"

"I know, but . . ."

"Katie, when Scott goes to all those out-of-town soccer games and tournaments, there must be girls hanging all over him afterward. I bet he takes some of them out for a hamburger or a Coke or something, but he never tells you about them because they aren't in the least bit important, right?"

Katie hadn't thought about this before, and now that she did, she wasn't sure she liked it.

"Well, maybe, but . . ."

"This is the exact same thing," Melissa insisted. "And that's why you have to go, and why you mustn't tell Scott where you're going. Make up some reason why you have to be away for a weekend. If your conscience pains you, you can tell him the truth later, and if he really loves you as much as you think he does, he'll understand."

"I guess I'll have to think about it some more," Katie said. "Now let's tackle that trig assignment, okay? Compared to my problem, it ought to be a piece of cake!"

After Melissa went home, Katie sat at her desk, staring at the red and gold foliage outside her window. She had to admit that Melissa had been very persuasive. But no matter what her friend said, Katie still couldn't believe it would be right to go to West Point without telling Scott.

On the other hand, if she *did* tell him and he didn't want her to accept Danny's invitation, Katie would be crushed. She wanted to go so badly!

For the next couple of days, Katie was tied in emotional knots, trying to come to a decision. Every time she spoke to Scott on the phone, she felt guilty about keeping the news from him, but she couldn't bring herself to mention it. Although Katie tried to convince herself that she didn't want to upset Scott while he was sick, she knew deep down inside that she was just being cowardly.

"Oh, Katie, for heaven's sake!" Melissa groaned when Katie confided her mixed feelings. "I simply don't understand you! The way you're acting, you'd think this was a matter of life and death, and it's not. I've said it before and I'll say it again—this West Point weekend is an *event,* not a real date. And besides, since when do you have to clear everything you do with Scott McAllister? You're his girlfriend, not his slave! Be independent! Stand on your own two feet!"

On Thursday, Kimmie was back in school, looking a little pale but otherwise completely recovered from her bout with the flu. Katie was delighted to see her, and to resume their daily chats at lunch.

As they sat down at their usual table, Katie planned to ask Kimmie's advice about her problem. But first she filled her friend in on what had been happening at school while she was sick, including the fact that the Thespians were putting on a production of "Brigadoon."

"I'm going to try out for the lead," Katie told her, "but Melissa is, too, which means that I probably won't get it."

"Why?" Kimmie asked. "Is she such a fantastic actress?"

"Well, I wouldn't say she's fantastic," Katie said. "At least, she didn't use to be. But somehow whenever we compete for anything, Melissa usually wins."

Kimmie paused to think for a moment, and then offered, "Sounds like a strange friendship if you ask me."

"It isn't really," Katie assured her. "Melissa's always been more competitive than I am, but other than that, we're very much alike."

"I guess I'll just have to take your word for it," Kimmie said. "Personally, from what I've seen of Melissa, I would have thought that the two of you couldn't be more different!"

"You don't like her very much, do you?" Katie blurted. The idea had never occurred to her before, and now that it had, it distressed her.

Kimmie looked uncomfortable. "Gee,

Katie, I hardly even *know* Melissa—none of the girls at Hillwood do except you. It's hard to like somebody you don't know." Changing the subject abruptly, she asked, "So how's the love of your life? You haven't mentioned Scott at all, and that's not like you."

"You're right, it's not," Katie said. "He's been out of school all week with the flu. We talk on the phone a lot, but he doesn't want anybody to visit him, so I haven't seen him since Monday." This seemed to be as good a time as any to bring up her West Point problem, so she began, "And speaking of Scott . . ."

Before Katie could continue, Carol brought her tray over to the table where she and Kimmie were sitting. "Hi, guys," she said. "Mind if I join you? Katie, don't forget about 'Brigadoon' tryouts after school today. I'm trying out for Meg, the comedy part, so I'm doing 'I Cain't Say No' from 'Oklahoma!' It's a really funny song. What's your audition piece going to be?"

" 'How Are Things in Glocca Morra?' from 'Finian's Rainbow,' " Katie told her.

"I remember when you played Sharon in the Thespians production of that show a couple of years ago," Kimmie said.

75

"Me too. You were really good, Katie," Carol added.

For the rest of their lunch period, the girls talked about past Thespians shows and the tryouts for "Brigadoon," so there was no opportunity for Katie to tell Kimmie about her brother's invitation. In fact, as the hours passed, she became so nervous at the thought of her upcoming audition that she forgot all about it.

In spite of her stage fright, Katie managed to get through her song without any trouble, and she actually enjoyed reading the lines of the scene Ms. Carletti, the Thespians advisor, had selected. Though several other girls auditioned for the part of Fiona, Melissa didn't show up. Katie wondered if that meant she had decided not to try out at all, or if she planned to attend Friday's auditions. Either way, she couldn't help feeling a little relieved that she hadn't had to perform in front of Melissa.

As Katie had promised, she called Scott the minute she got home to tell him how tryouts had gone.

"I knew you'd do fine," he said when she finished. "I told Melissa she shouldn't even bother trying out because I was sure you'd get the part."

"Melissa?" Katie repeated, startled. "Did you speak to her today?"

"Yeah—she came over after school and brought me some frozen yogurt."

Katie frowned. "I thought you said you didn't want any visitors."

"Well, I didn't," Scott said, "but I guess nobody told Melissa. She just rang the doorbell and Mom let her in. We had a really interesting talk."

"That's nice. What did you talk about?" Katie asked, trying to ignore a sudden sharp stab of jealousy.

"Oh, a lot of different things—the tryouts and school, stuff like that. Actually, Melissa did most of the talking." He paused. "You know, I guess I was wrong about her. She's not an airhead after all. I just didn't realize what a hard time she's had. She's still pretty upset about her parents' divorce, though she tries not to show it. And she says that except for you and me, the kids at school haven't been all that friendly. I get the impression that Melissa's kind of lonely."

"You're probably right," Katie admitted,

immediately ashamed of herself for feeling jealous of her friend even for a moment. "And if she is, it's partly my fault. Except for the Teen Scene interview, I haven't spent very much time with her lately."

"Don't be so hard on yourself, Katie," Scott said. "Melissa thinks you're the greatest— she kept saying so over and over. Listen, I've got a doctor's appointment in a few minutes so I have to go. But if he gives me a clean bill of health, I'll see you in school tomorrow."

"Good!" Katie said, smiling. "I've missed you an awful lot."

"I've missed you too. Bye, Katie."

"Bye."

As Katie hung up the phone in the hall, she wondered why they hadn't exchanged their usual "I love you's." But she quickly forgot about that as she realized that once again she hadn't had a chance to tell Scott about her invitation to West Point.

Then she shook her head and sighed. *Who am I trying to kid, anyway?* she said to herself. *I didn't tell him because I'm afraid he'll tell me not to go.*

Katie remembered what Melissa had said earlier that week about being independent and standing on her own two feet. *She's right,* Katie thought. *I have to make up my own mind, not depend on somebody else to do it for me.*

"It's *my* decision, after all," she said aloud, "and I'm going to make it right now!"

As Katie spoke, her mother came out of the den. "Did you say something, dear?" she asked.

"Just talking to myself," Katie replied. "By the way," she added casually, "I don't think I mentioned that in Danny's letter, he invited me to visit him at the Point."

"No, you didn't," Mrs. O'Connor said. "What fun! But why didn't you say anything about it before?"

"Well, I wasn't sure if I was going or not," Katie told her. "But now I am. I'm just about to write back to Danny and tell him yes."

"That's wonderful," her mother said. "When will it be?"

"I don't know yet, but it'll probably be soon. Danny said his roommate will write and give me all the details."

As Katie started up the stairs, she heard her mother say, "I can't wait to tell your father. He'll be so pleased!"

Once Katie was in her room, she sat down

at her desk and quickly wrote a short note
to her brother:

Dear Danny,

See? I do remember who you are! I'm
really sorry I haven't answered your letter until now, but you know me. I've been
awfully busy with schoolwork, soccer,
and other stuff like that.

Thanks so much for the invitation. I'd
love to come up for a weekend. Please
tell Ben Anderson that I look forward to
hearing from him, and to meeting him in
person. And of course, I can't wait to see
you.

Take care up there!

Much love,
Katie

After she sealed the envelope and addressed it, Katie hurried out of the house
and dropped her letter in the mailbox on the
corner. There! She'd done it! And now that
she had, she was sure that it would be much
easier to tell Scott about her plans.

Chapter Seven

The cast list for "Brigadoon" wasn't posted until the following Tuesday, and when Katie and Scott approached the bulletin board that morning, she was almost afraid to look. But when she did, Katie let out a squeal of delight. "I can't believe this!" she cried, clutching Scott's arm. "Carol's playing Meg, and I'm Fiona!"

Scott gave her a hug. "Congratulations, Katie," he said. "I don't know why you're so surprised. I never doubted for a minute that you'd get the part. Next stop, Broadway!"

"Oh, sure!" Katie scoffed, giggling. "My name will be right up there in lights, along with Aunt Sheila's."

"That's right—I'd forgotten that your aunt's an actress," Scott said. "I guess creative talent must run in the O'Connor family."

Katie grinned. "Thanks, but I'm afraid you're wrong. Aunt Sheila's my mother's sister, not my father's. It's the Sheridans who are the creative types—the O'Connors are military all the way. I know Aunt Sheila will be pleased when she finds out I'll be playing the same part she played a few years back." Rummaging in her purse, she found a pencil and began writing down the rehearsal schedule on a page of her trig notebook.

"Looks like you're going to be pretty busy for a while," Scott observed. "Beginning next week, there's a rehearsal after school almost every day. It's a good thing soccer season's almost over, or you wouldn't have been able to be in the show."

"Yeah, I know. And to think I was actually looking forward to having some free time for a change!" Katie said, shaking her head.

"Think you'll be able to fit me into your busy schedule, Miss Sarah Bernhardt?" Scott teased as they walked down the hall to their first class.

Reaching out to take his hand, Katie laughed. "Don't be silly! Of course I will. I'll always have time for you!"

For the rest of the day, Katie really did feel like a Broadway star. All her friends, particularly her fellow Thespians, congratulated her on landing the leading role in the musical.

"I can't wait to see you up there onstage with the mists of Brigadoon swirling around you," Melissa told Katie as she drove her home after soccer practice that afternoon. "I know you'll make a wonderful Fiona."

Katie smiled. "Thanks, Melissa. But if you'd decided to try out, I'd most likely be congratulating *you* instead of the other way around."

"Possibly," Melissa agreed. "I'm glad I didn't, though. I mean, I'd hate to be tied up in rehearsals for the rest of the year." Glancing over at Katie, she added, "How does Scott feel about that?"

"Oh, he's happy for me," Katie said. "That's one of the things I love about Scott—he's so understanding. I'm sure he'll understand about my trip to West Point, too."

"Then you're definitely going?"

Katie nodded. "I wrote to Danny last week saying I would. I'm just waiting for his roommate to set the date, and then I'll tell Scott."

"Suit yourself, Katie," Melissa said with a shrug. "I've told you a million times what I think about that, but I certainly can't force you to follow my advice. Who knows? Maybe Scott really *will* understand why you've accepted a blind date with your brother's roommate. He'll probably never even let you know how badly you've hurt his feelings because he won't want to spoil your fun."

She slowed the red Porsche to a stop in front of Katie's house. "Well, here we are. See you tomorrow, Katie."

"Yeah—see you. Thanks for the lift, Melissa," Katie said as she got out of the car.

Rather than going inside immediately, she decided to take a walk while she mulled over what Melissa had just said. *The last thing I want to do is hurt Scott,* Katie thought as she ambled slowly down the tree-lined street. *Maybe honesty isn't always the best policy if it makes somebody unhappy. I guess it wouldn't be too terrible if I didn't tell him after all. . . .*

* * *

A few days later, Katie found a handsome gray envelope with the West Point crest waiting for her when she got home from school. It was a letter from Ben Anderson. Taking it up to her bedroom, she opened it eagerly and began to read.

Dear Katie,

I'm real glad to hear that you can come to the Point. Are you free the weekend of November 4? There's a parade at eleven o'clock Saturday morning (Danny and I will be in it), and in the afternoon at the football game we'll watch Army beat Cornell. We can have dinner somewhere nice and maybe see a movie Saturday night if you like.

I've seen your picture and heard a lot about you from your brother, but knowing Danny, I bet he hasn't told you much about me. So here goes.

I'm five feet eleven, brown hair, brown eyes, and kind of average-looking. I grew up on a ranch in Montana so I'm pretty good at riding, roping, and stuff like that. (Don't get much chance to do that here in upstate New York, though!) I'm sort of shy and I'm not much of a talker, but if you poke me, I'll probably rustle up a sentence or two— maybe even more.

I just read this over and I think it sounds pretty boring. Sorry, but it's all I can think of to say about myself.

Danny says you'll be staying at the Thayer Hotel, so if you can come the weekend of the 4th, let one of us know real quick. We'll give the information to the cadet hostess so she can reserve a room for you with another girl.

Best wishes,

Ben Anderson

Company D-1

Katie smiled as she finished reading Ben's letter. She thought he sounded nice—not very exciting and not at all romantic, but then Katie wasn't looking for excitement and romance anymore. Glancing at the calendar on her desk, she realized that the weekend of the fourth was only two weeks away.

Just imagine! she said to herself as she went downstairs to show the letter to her mother. *I've been dreaming of a West Point weekend practically all my life, and in two weeks, my dream is going to come true!*

Katie found her mother sitting at her computer in the den and staring vacantly into space.

"You look like you're in another world. Am I interrupting a train of thought?" she asked, giving Mrs. O'Connor a gentle pat on the head.

"Careful, Katie," her mother warned, only half joking. "If you addle my poor brain, it'll mess up the storyline that's stored in there and then I'll have to start all over from scratch."

Peering at the computer screen, Katie asked, "What are you working on? *Countdown to Terror*?"

Mrs. O'Connor nodded. "Yes. The murderer has been stalking the heroine for three chapters now, and Detective Russo hasn't found a single clue. I just realized that if I don't give him some clue in the next few pages, the poor girl won't last until the end of chapter four. Did you want me for something?"

"I just wanted to show you this letter from Ben Anderson, Danny's roommate," Katie said, handing it to her. "He's invited me to West Point for the weekend of November fourth. Is that all right with you and Dad?"

Mrs. O'Connor skimmed the letter, then smiled at her. "Ben sounds like a very nice boy. As far as I'm concerned, there's no problem with that weekend, and I'm sure your father will have no objection either. He's very much in favor of this trip, you know."

Katie made a face. "I certainly do. I think Dad's hoping that I'll dump Scott for a long-distance romance with some West Point cadet, but that's not going to happen."

"Don't be so hard on your father, Katie," Mrs. O'Connor said gently. "He loves you very much and he only wants what's best for you."

Changing the subject, she went on, "Now let's talk about your travel arrangements. You'd better drop a note to Ben tonight and ask him to see about getting you a room at the Thayer for Friday and Saturday nights. Better yet, why don't you phone him this evening?"

"Phone him?" Katie echoed. "Gee, Mom, I

don't know . . . I mean, I'd feel weird calling a guy I've never even met."

"Well, you'll be meeting him in two weeks," her mother pointed out. "It might be nice to get acquainted over the phone first. But if you feel funny about it, call your brother. Let's see—I'll book your flight, and either Dad or I will take you to the airport on Friday afternoon. Unless you'd rather ask Scott to drive you," she added.

"He won't be able to," Katie said quickly. "There's a soccer game that night in Athens, the last game of the season. The team will have to leave right after school."

Mrs. O'Connor glanced at her. "This weekend hasn't caused any trouble between you and Scott, has it, Katie?"

"No, Mom, no trouble at all," Katie told her truthfully. She was about to leave when she suddenly remembered about the play. "Oh, by the way, Mom, I almost forgot to tell you—they posted the cast list for 'Brigadoon' today, and guess what? I got the lead!"

"Katie! That's wonderful! I'm so proud of you." Mrs. O'Connor ran over to Katie and gave her a big hug. "I'll call Sheila tonight right after supper—I know she'll be thrilled! And speaking of supper," she added, checking her watch, "how about giving me a hand getting it ready? Your father will be home soon, and so will Willie. They'll both be hungry as bears, and I haven't even thought about what we're going to eat."

After supper that evening, Katie was sitting in her room, trying to decide whether to write a note to Ben or call Danny when she heard Willie yelling, "*Katieee!* Aunt Sheila's on the phone and she wants to talk to you!"

Always eager to talk to her favorite aunt, Katie ran out into the hall and picked up the receiver of the upstairs phone. "Hi, Aunt Sheila," she said. "How are you? I haven't spoken to you in ages!"

"And whose fault is that, I'd like to know?" Aunt Sheila said in that husky voice Katie loved. "Why didn't you phone and tell me your exciting news, you naughty girl? I had to hear about 'Brigadoon' from your mother just now. Congratulations, Fiona! What are the dates? I'm opening in a new play soon, but it's a limited engagement. If I can possibly manage it, I intend to fly down and see your show."

"Really? Oh, that would be super!" Katie exclaimed happily. She gave her aunt the information, then said, "So tell me about this play you're in."

"It's called 'The Grass Is Greener' and it's a marvelous comedy by a tremendously talented young playwright," Aunt Sheila said. "We open next week. Actually, Katie, I have a proposition for you. Your mom tells me you're going to West Point the weekend of November fourth. How would you like to fly to New York on the third, see the show, and spend the night with me? I could pick you up at the airport Friday afternoon, drive you to the Point early Saturday morning, and even pick you up from the Point on Sunday to take you back to the airport."

"Oh, wow!" Katie breathed. "That sounds absolutely fabulous! If Mom and Dad will let me, I'd love it!"

"I thought the idea might appeal to you," her aunt said with a throaty chuckle. "Let me speak to them about it now. I'm sure I can talk them into it."

"Thanks *so* much, Aunt Sheila!" Katie cried. Still holding the receiver, she ran to the head of the stairs and hollered, "Mom, Dad, pick up the phone! Aunt Sheila wants to talk to you about something very important!"

Katie eavesdropped unashamedly on the conversation between her parents and her aunt, and when both Colonel and Mrs. O'Connor agreed to Aunt Sheila's plan, she let out a whoop of delight. This weekend was going to be even more wonderful than she had ever imagined!

As soon as they all hung up, Katie phoned Danny to give him the news.

"Sounds great," he said. "I'll tell Ben you'll only need a room for Saturday night. Better yet, why don't you tell him yourself? He's right here."

"Listen, Danny, I don't think—" Katie began, but before she could finish, a deep voice said, "Hi, Katie. This is Ben Anderson."

"Uh—hi, Ben. I—I got your letter today," Katie stammered. "Thanks for writing to me. The parade and the football game and everything sound like a lot of fun. I'm looking forward to meeting you."

"Me too," Ben said. "I mean, I'm looking forward to meeting *you*—I've already met me . . ." Katie couldn't help giggling, and Ben mumbled, "Oh, boy, did that ever sound stupid!"

"No it didn't," Katie assured him quickly. "I guess maybe you're as nervous about talking to me as I am about talking to you, right?"

She heard him heave a long, gusty sigh. "That's about the size of it. Like I said in that letter, I'm not much of a talker."

"Well, when we finally meet, I'll be sure to poke you a couple of times to get you going," Katie said.

Ben laughed. "Okay. But not in the ribs, please—I'm real ticklish."

Katie laughed too. "I'll be sure to remember that!"

"So I guess Danny and I will be seeing you on the morning of the fourth then," Ben said. "I'll get you a room at the Thayer for that night. After you check in, do you think you can call for us at Grant Hall at ten o'clock?"

"Sure. No problem," Katie replied.

There was a long pause. Finally Ben said, "Well—uh—nice talking to you, Katie."

"Nice talking to you, too. Give my love to Danny."

As Katie hung up, she was glad she'd called. She liked the slight western twang in Ben's speech, and his sense of humor reminded her of Danny's. So what if he was a little shy? She was sure that once they got to know each other, he'd loosen up and they'd have a pleasant time together. It would be almost like having two big brothers at West Point instead of one!

Chapter Eight

It seemed to Katie that the next week sped by like a videotape on fast-forward. The Blue Devils won their last match of the season, and rehearsals for "Brigadoon" immediately took the place of soccer practice most days after school. On Katie's one free afternoon, her mother took her clothes shopping because Katie didn't own anything suitable for November weather in the north.

"I never see you anymore, Katie," Scott complained at Kimmie's Halloween party. He and Katie, both dressed as pirates, were slow-dancing to a dreamy tune. "This is the first time we've been out together since our movie date last Saturday night, and then you had to get home early to study for some test."

"I know," Katie sighed, "and I'm really sorry. But Ms. Carletti's a real slave-driver— 'Brigadoon' has a huge cast, and she wants everyone in it to be absolutely perfect. If we don't know all our lines and all the songs by heart when we start run-throughs next week, Carletti will hit the ceiling."

"Well, at least you don't have to rehearse on weekends," Scott said, holding her close and nuzzling her ear, "or else I'd never get to see you at all. Oh, that reminds me—we're going to Ted Stoddard's party next Saturday night. Write it down on your calendar, Katie, so you don't forget. It ought to be a real blast."

Katie stiffened in his arms. "Next Saturday night? You mean November fourth?"

"That's the date," Scott told her. "I'll pick you up around seven-thirty, okay?"

"Oh, Scott, I can't go!" Katie said.

Stepping back, he looked down at her with a frown on his handsome face. "Why not? Don't tell me your father's making waves again."

"No, that's not it. I can't go because I won't be here." Katie took a deep breath. If she was ever going to tell Scott about her West Point weekend, this was the time to do it. Deciding to ease into it gradually, she said, "I hope you're not going to be too upset, but my Aunt Sheila's new play just opened on Broadway, and she's invited me to see it next Friday night. I'm flying to New York that afternoon—Ms. Carletti said it would be okay for me to skip rehearsal. I'll see the show, spend the night with her, and then—"

"Hey, that's really cool!" Scott interrupted, smiling now. "Why would I be upset? There'll be plenty of other parties, but an opportunity like this doesn't come along every day."

"I know," Katie said. "I'm very excited about it. But that's not all, Scott. On Saturday Aunt Sheila's taking me to—"

"Okay, you two lovebirds, break it up!" A tall, thin ghost who turned out to be Johnnie Warden tapped Scott on the shoulder. "I've always wanted to dance with a pirate." Scott grinned and spread his arms wide. "Not you, McAllister. The *pretty* one!"

Melissa, dressed as a French can-can dancer, joined them just then. Katie was glad that Kimmie had invited her to the party, hoping it meant that the girls were finally becoming friends. "Poor Scott! I guess that means you're stuck with me," Melissa said with a wink at Katie.

The music changed to a pulsing rock-and-roll beat, and Johnnie grabbed Katie's hand. As the two couples began to dance, Katie thought, *Well at least I tried to tell Scott the truth, I really did.*

But she knew perfectly well that she wouldn't have such a good opportunity again.

When Katie woke up the following Saturday morning, it took a few groggy minutes before she realized that she was in her aunt's Manhattan apartment and not in her own familiar bed at home. Suddenly all the exciting memories of yesterday came flooding back—the flight to New York, dinner with Aunt Sheila at a charming French restaurant, and best of all, her aunt's stellar performance in "The Grass Is Greener." Katie had laughed until she cried, and during the curtain calls she clapped so long and hard that her hands stung and her arms ached.

Now the rest of Katie's weekend lay ahead

of her. Eager to start the day, she leaped out of bed, splashed cold water on her face, and brushed her teeth. Katie had just finished putting on her new slate-blue corduroys and white turtleneck sweater and was brushing the tangles out of her long brown hair when she heard a tap at her door.

"Come on in, Aunt Sheila," she called out.

"Well, aren't you the early bird!" her aunt said, stepping into the room. "Considering how late we stayed up last night, I thought I'd have to blast you out of bed, but here you are, all dressed and ready to go." In snug-fitting jeans and a bulky Irish fisherman knit sweater and with her burnished gold hair hanging loose, she looked even prettier than she had onstage the night before, Katie thought.

"My stuff's all packed, too," Katie told her. "Except for my hairbrush, and I'll be through with it as soon as I tame this disgusting mop of mine. What time do you think we ought to leave?"

Sheila glanced at her watch. "Not for about forty-five minutes. You'll have plenty of time for a nice nourishing breakfast." When Katie made a face, she laughed. "I'll make a deal with you. If you eat every bite, I'll give you the benefit of my professional expertise and help you with your hair and makeup."

Grinning, Katie said, "You're on! I need all the help I can get."

After Katie had polished off her cereal, orange juice, and hot cocoa, Sheila sat down in front of her dressing table and began to work her magic. When she had finished, Katie stared wide-eyed at her reflection in the mirror.

"Wow! That's amazing!" she exclaimed. "I look so much prettier, and a lot older, too. I bet my own brother won't recognize me! I love the false eyelashes—they look so natural. But are you sure they won't fall off or anything?"

"It's highly unlikely," Sheila said with a smile. "Now if you'll get your jacket and overnight bag, we'd better be on our way. West Point is only about an hour's drive from here, but if we run into traffic, it could take longer, and you don't want to keep that handsome cadet waiting."

"I don't know if Ben's handsome or not," Katie said as she put on her down jacket, "and it doesn't really matter. Like I told you last night, I'm going steady with a boy back

100

home." Remembering what Melissa had said, she added, "As far as I'm concerned, this isn't even a date. It's an *event*."

Sheila chuckled. "Well, whatever you call it, you don't want to be late for it. Come on, Katie—let's hit the road."

Little more than an hour later after a scenic drive along the Hudson River, Sheila's gray BMW came to a stop in front of the Thayer Hotel, an elegant old stone building surrounded by shrubbery and set back among tall trees glowing with the red and gold hues of late autumn.

As Katie and her aunt entered the lobby and approached the front desk, Katie tried to ignore the butterflies that suddenly began fluttering in the pit of her stomach; now that she was actually here, she almost wished she hadn't come, but it was much too late to turn back.

After the clerk confirmed Katie's reservation and handed her the key to room 221, Sheila gave her a hug. "It looks as if everything's under control, so I'll be leaving now. I'll be back to pick you up around two o'clock tomorrow afternoon. Have a super time, sweetie."

"Thanks for everything, Aunt Sheila," Katie said. She walked her aunt to the door and waited until she drove away. Then, still doing battle with the butterflies, she headed for room 221.

As Katie let herself in, she saw a tall, pretty blonde sitting on one of the twin beds. "Hi! I'm your roommate, Cindy Mayfair from Tarrytown, New York," the girl said, getting up and coming over to Katie, hand outstretched. Her friendly smile immediately made Katie feel at ease.

"Hi, Cindy. I'm Katie O'Connor, currently from Fort Benning, Georgia." Katie put down her suitcase and the two girls shook hands.

"Currently?" Cindy repeated.

"I'm an army brat," Katie told her. "So far, we've moved five times."

Cindy cocked her head and looked Katie up and down. "For an Army brat, you look pretty normal. So who's your date?"

"Ben Anderson. He's my brother's roommate, but I've never met him. This is my first trip to West Point, and I'm really excited," Katie said. "What about you?"

"My guy's Charlie Edwards. We're from the same hometown and we've known each other since fifth grade. I've been here twice before, and every time I come I feel kind of a glow. For a while I even thought about becoming a cadet, but I decided against it. I don't think I could hack it."

"Me either," Katie agreed. "I really admire the girls who do, though." She looked at her watch. "Listen, Cindy, I'm supposed to meet Ben and my brother at Grant Hall in about fifteen minutes. Can you tell me how to get there?"

"I'll do better than that," Cindy said. "I'm meeting Charlie there too, and I have a car so I'll drive you. Do you want to freshen up or anything before we leave? Not that you need it," she added. "You look great. I bet Ben Anderson will flip out when he sees you. This could be the start of a great romance!"

"No way," Katie said, laughing. "That's not why I came here, and besides, I'm sure Ben just thinks of me as Danny's kid sister. Neither of us is looking for romance, believe me."

"Too bad," Cindy said cheerfully. "Oh, well, you'll have fun anyway. Just give me a minute to get my coat, and we'll take off."

Chapter Nine

Grant Hall was barely a mile away from the hotel, and the girls walked into the huge reception area on the dot of ten o'clock. Katie's jitters returned full force as she followed Cindy across the room to a soldier seated behind a desk.

After Cindy gave the man Charlie's name, Katie told him that she was calling for Ben Anderson from Company D-1. "And my brother Danny, too," she added nervously. The soldier looked up at her, obviously waiting for her to say something more. "Oh, sorry—that's Danny O'Connor," she told him, blushing with embarrassment.

104

"He must think I'm an idiot," she whispered to Cindy as they left the desk and sat down on one of the couches.

"Don't worry about it," Cindy replied, smiling. "I'm sure he's used to nervous girls by now. The first time I called for Charlie, I was practically a basket case. I've known him forever, but all of a sudden I couldn't remember his last name!"

She went on to tell Katie some other funny things that had happened on her first visit to West Point, and as Katie listened and laughed, she felt her tension gradually ebbing away.

Suddenly Cindy stood up. "Here comes Charlie now," she said. "And unless I miss my guess, the two guys right behind him belong to you."

Katie stood too, admiring the three cadets walking briskly toward them. They looked so trim and handsome in their gray uniforms trimmed in black and matching visored hats! As Cindy ran to greet a husky, blond young man, Katie raced straight into her tall, dark-haired brother's arms.

"Oh, Danny, it's so good to see you!" she cried, then let out a shriek when he picked her up and spun her around. "Put me down, you big ox!" Katie gasped, giggling.

"I was just giving you the West Point Welcome," Danny said with a grin as he set her back on her feet. "It's good to see you too, little sister. Come to think of it, you're not so little anymore," he added. "Pretty soon I won't be able to get you off the ground."

Katie gave him a mock scowl. "Are you telling me I'm getting fat?"

"Well, maybe it's just that down jacket . . ." Danny teased, and ducked the punch Katie aimed at him.

"Don't you listen to him, Katie. You look perfect," Ben Anderson said.

Katie had been so happy to see her brother that she had almost forgotten about Ben, and now she really looked at him for the first time. He wasn't a hunk, but he was nice-looking, with twinkly brown eyes and a slightly lopsided grin.

"Thanks, Ben," Katie said, smiling at him. "I guess we can consider ourselves introduced, since it doesn't look as if Danny's going to do the honors."

"Sorry about that," Danny said. "Katie,

Ben. Ben, Katie. Better late than never, right?"

"Well done, Danny," Katie joked. "Maybe you'll make military attachésome day."

Just then Cindy and Charlie came over to them. After more introductions and some casual conversation, Danny said, "Listen, girls, we have to get into formation for the parade, so why don't you go to the Plain and snag a couple of seats down front?"

"Good idea," Cindy said. "We'll stay where we are after the parade so you can find us." She gave Charlie a quick kiss, then said, "Come on, Katie, we can walk. The Plain— that's the parade ground—is only about a block from here."

As the girls walked the short distance, Cindy said, "Ben's really cute, and so is your brother. How come Danny doesn't have a date this weekend? Is he seeing anybody? Not that I'm interested," she added with a grin, "just nosy."

"Danny's girlfriend goes to college in the south," Katie told her. "I don't think she can afford to come up here very often."

"So what do you think of Ben Anderson?"

Katie shrugged. "He seems very nice."

"No romantic sparks?" Cindy teased.

Katie just shook her head, smiling. "Afraid not. I'm dating a terrific guy back home, and that's all the romance I need."

Although a lot of people had turned out to see the parade, Katie and Cindy were able to find seats in the third row of the bleachers. Soon the regiments marched onto the Plain to the stirring military music of the Academy band, and Katie felt a shiver run up and down her spine. It was so thrilling to see hundreds of cadets marching in their dress gray uniforms and white cross-belts, wearing their plumed "tarbucket" hats with the West Point crest in front. The officers wore maroon sashes and carried sabers, while the others marched with rifles on their shoulders. Cindy picked out Charlie immediately, but though Katie searched and searched, she couldn't find either Danny or Ben—in that sea of faces, all the cadets, male and female, looked alike.

When the parade was finally over and the rest of the spectators began leaving the bleachers, Katie and Cindy remained where they were. Not long afterward, Charlie, Ben, and Danny joined them.

"So how did you like the show?" Ben asked Katie.

Still glowing with excitement, she gushed, "Oh, it was fabulous! I've never seen anything like it. The flags, the music, the drilling—when all of you marched off the field, I wanted to follow you to some distant land!"

Danny groaned. "You'll have to excuse my sister, Ben. Katie gets carried away sometimes. She even gets this way when she sees a movie or reads an exciting book."

Smiling at Katie, Ben said, "I think that's nice. I like people who aren't afraid to let their emotions run away with them."

"Thanks, Ben," Katie said, and made a face at her brother. "Unlike some people I could name, *you're* an officer and a gentleman!"

"Well, I'm a long way from being an officer, but I always try to act like a gentleman," Ben told her seriously.

After lunch, Katie, Ben, and Danny went with Cindy and Charlie to the football stadium. As soon as the two couples were seated, Danny excused himself. He was going to sit with some of his friends, "so you two can get to know each other without Big Brother looking over your shoulders," he said to Katie. "I probably won't see you again today, kid, but I'll meet you at the Thayer for breakfast tomorrow morning around ten. Have fun!"

As the Black Knights of West Point took the field against Cornell, Ben pointed out some of the Academy's outstanding players, but Katie was more interested in Army's mascots, two mules that were ridden by cadets.

"When my dad was at West Point, they only had one mule," she told Ben. "He tells these wild stories about how the midshipmen from the Naval Academy used to steal it right before the Army-Navy game. Then the cadets would kidnap Navy's goat."

"I had an uncle who was in on that a long time ago," Charlie put in. "He told me how they managed it, but it's a deep, dark secret. My lips are sealed." He made a zipping motion across his mouth for emphasis.

"Do you think you'll win the Army-Navy game this year?" Cindy asked.

"We'd better," Ben said, grinning. "I have a

buddy at the Naval Academy who sends me a letter every week and all it says is 'Beat Army.' If we lose, I'll never hear the end of it!"

Unfortunately, after putting up a good fight, the Black Knights lost that day's game to Cornell, but the defeat didn't dampen Katie's spirits. She was having too good a time, and when Ben suggested a walking tour of the Point after the game, she readily agreed.

"You guys go ahead," Charlie said. "Cindy and I are going to the snack bar near Grant Hall to drown our sorrows in a couple of Cokes. But how about catching a movie tonight? There's an old Abbott and Costello film playing—something about a haunted house. I think it starts at seven-thirty."

"Sounds great," Katie said, and Ben nodded.

"If you meet us at the snack bar around six, Katie, I'll give you a ride back to the hotel so we can change," Cindy suggested.

"She'll be there," Ben promised. Offering his arm to Katie, he said, "Ready for the grand tour, Ms. O'Connor? We'd better get a move on because it's getting dark, and it also looks as if it might start to rain."

Katie smiled at him. "Lead on, Cadet Anderson!"

Arm in arm, they skirted the parade ground and headed in the direction of the river and Trophy Point. As they walked, Ben kept up a running commentary that Katie found fascinating.

"That big gray building up there is the Cadet Chapel," he told her, pointing out a huge Gothic structure in the distance. "We won't have time to do it justice today, but maybe we'll see it the next time you come. It has these incredible stained glass windows that are really spectacular when the sun shines through them. Just going in there makes me realize that I'm an integral part of that Long Gray Line stretching all the way back to 1802."

"For somebody who doesn't talk much, you certainly have a lot to say about West Point," Katie teased. "And I haven't even poked you." Suddenly aware that she was still holding Ben's arm, she released it.

"It means a whole lot to me," Ben admitted. "I'm going to train as an astronaut later on. The first place I want to get to is Mars."

"Oh, take me with you!" Katie cried. "Ever

since I was a little kid, I wanted to find out if there was life up there. Do you think there is?"

"Could be. And even if there isn't, there are millions of other galaxies to explore. I'm willing to bet that there must be intelligent life out there somewhere."

"What about extraterrestrials here on Earth?" Katie asked. "Do you think we have any E.T.s prowling around?"

"Could be." Ben narrowed his eyes and bared his teeth. "What proof do you have that I'm really from Montana? I just might be West Point's first alien cadet!"

Giggling, Katie said, "If you want to scare me, you'll have to do better than that!"

They were approaching Trophy Point high above the Hudson River, and Ben showed her the Battle Monument dedicated to the Union soldiers who died in the Civil War, the cemetery where General Custer was buried, and the little chapel. Katie was impressed by Ben's knowledge and enthusiasm, though by then it was so dark that she could hardly see a thing.

They had just started to retrace their steps when the rain began. It was just a sprinkle at first, but it soon turned into a downpour.

Ben grabbed Katie's hand, and they ran the rest of the way to the snack bar, laughing and sputtering. By the time they were safely inside, Katie's hair was hanging in sodden strings around her face. Forgetting about the makeup Aunt Sheila had so artistically applied, she found a tissue in her purse and hastily mopped her wet face. When she had finished, Ben took one look at her and laughed harder than ever.

"What's so funny?" Katie demanded, though she was laughing too.

"This!" He carefully plucked one of her false eyelashes off her cheek. "Don't get me wrong—I like girls who wear their eyelashes in strange places."

He handed it back to her with a flourish, and Katie said between giggles, "Thank you, kind sir. When you see me tonight at the movies, I'll be wearing this on my nose!"

Later that evening as Ben and Katie followed Cindy and Charlie into the movie theater, Ben whispered, "You know something, Katie? With or without false eyelashes on your nose, I like your looks. In fact, I like everything about you."

Katie murmured, "Thank you, Ben. I like you, too." *Maybe I'm beginning to like you a little too much,* she thought.

Feeling suddenly confused and uncomfortable, Katie kept her hands folded in her lap during the movie except when she reached for popcorn from the bucket Ben held.

When the film was over, Charlie and Cindy said they wanted to take a little walk before Cindy and Katie would head back to the hotel. The rain had stopped, and the moon shone brightly from a cloudless sky. As they ambled off, their arms around each other, Ben took Katie's hand.

"Why don't we take a walk too?" he suggested.

In spite of her mixed feelings, Katie could hardly refuse without seeming rude. While the two of them walked down the street hand in hand, she kept up a steady stream of nervous chatter about the funny movie they had just seen, but Ben hardly said a word.

In the shadows beneath a tall old tree, he suddenly stood still. Putting his hands on Katie's shoulders, Ben turned her to face him. And then, very gently, he kissed her.

"I've been wanting to do that ever since we

115

met," he said softly just before he kissed her again. Ben's lips were soft and warm on hers, and for a moment Katie felt herself responding.

But only for a moment. *What's the matter with me?* she thought as she quickly drew away. *This is all wrong! I'm in love with Scott, not Ben Anderson. So why did I let Ben kiss me? I must be a terrible person!*

Ben immediately released her, and in the moonlight filtering through the leaves above them Katie could see how distressed he looked. "I'm sorry, Katie," he said sincerely. "I shouldn't have done that—we haven't even known each other for one whole day! I told you this morning that I always try to act like a gentleman. Well, tonight I didn't, and I wouldn't blame you if you slapped me or something."

Katie's heart went out to him. "Oh, Ben, I'm not angry," she said. "In fact, I'm flattered. You just took me by surprise, that's all." *And I took myself by surprise, too,* she thought.

"Do you think you could kind of pretend this never happened?" Ben asked hesitantly as they began walking back to where Cindy had parked her car. "I mean, can you give me another chance? If you'll come to the Point again someday, I'll finish that guided tour—in daylight this time." Glancing at her shyly, he added, "And if you come, I promise I won't kiss you again unless you tell me you want me to."

"We'll see," Katie murmured. But since Scott was the only boy for her, she knew that as much as she liked Ben Anderson, she had to put him out of her mind forever.

Chapter Ten

Katie did a lot of heavy thinking on the plane ride back home that Sunday afternoon, and by Monday morning everything was crystal-clear in her mind.

She knew that she had made a lot of mistakes over the past few weeks, beginning with accepting Danny's invitation to West Point. Katie's second mistake was concealing the whole truth from Scott about where she was going, and her third was not telling Ben Anderson that she was dating a boy back home.

There's nothing I can do about number one or number three, Katie told herself as she walked up the steps to Hillwood High. *But from now on I'm going to be completely honest with Scott. I'm going to tell him all about my weekend today. I'll even tell him about Ben. I'm sure he'll understand that it didn't really mean anything at all. And besides, I'll never see Ben again.*

Katie knew that her confession wasn't going to be easy. It wasn't the sort of thing you could mention casually in class or in the halls, so she decided to ask Scott to meet her after school. Since soccer season was over, he wouldn't have practice, and there was no "Brigadoon" rehearsal scheduled until Tuesday. They would drive out to Shadow Lake, where Katie would explain everything.

Scott was already in his seat when Katie walked into Mr. Stevenson's World Literature class, and her heart leaped at the sight of his handsome face. She smiled and waved and he waved back. With all sorts of thoughts churning in her head, Katie found it impossible to concentrate on what the teacher was saying about "Hamlet," and breathed a sigh of relief when one of the kids was called on to give an oral report on the movie of Shakespeare's play starring Laurence Olivier. Katie had seen the film many times on videotape, so she was able to tune out without missing anything vital.

As soon as class was over, Katie hurried out of the room and waited for Scott by the door.

"Hi," she said when he emerged, standing on tiptoe to give him a kiss on the cheek. "Long time no see!"

"Yeah. How was the play?" Scott asked.

"Oh, great," Katie said enthusiastically as they began walking down the hall. "It was terribly funny, and Aunt Sheila was fantastic. I'll tell you all about it, but not right now. Could we drive out to Shadow Lake after school? There's something very important I want to talk to you about, not just the play."

Scott nodded. "I'll meet you in the parking lot." Quickening his pace, he added, "Look, I have to stop by the office for something before my next class. See you around two-thirty, okay?"

Katie gazed after him as he strode down the hall without a backward glance. Scott certainly hadn't seemed very glad to see her.

Was something bothering him? Or was it just her guilty conscience?

For the rest of the morning, Katie's feeling of unease grew. It wasn't just Scott who was acting weird. When she spoke to her friends, they seemed oddly uncomfortable, and several times she saw small groups of kids she knew whispering together and giving her funny looks.

"Kimmie, what's going on?" Katie asked her friend at noon as they carried their lunch trays to their usual table and sat down.

Kimmie avoided her eyes, focusing instead on her bowl of chili. "What do you mean?"

Katie frowned. "If there's one thing that drives me up the wall, it's people who answer a question with a question! I mean why is everybody acting so peculiar around me today?"

"Are they?"

"You just did it again!" Katie groaned. "If you don't know, *say* you don't know, but please stop beating around the bush."

There was a long pause while Kimmie continued to stare at her food. Finally she looked up. "I *do* know, but I'm not sure if I should tell you or not." She sighed. "I mean, you're bound to find out sooner or later, so I guess it would be better if you heard it from me. On the other hand—"

"*Kimberly Martin,* if you value your life, *tell me!*" Katie exploded.

"Okay, but first promise me you won't be like those ancient Greek kings who killed the messengers who brought them bad news," Kimmie said.

Really worried now, Katie said, "I promise." Suddenly she had an awful feeling that she knew what the bad news was. "It's 'Brigadoon,' isn't it? Ms. Carletti gave the lead to somebody else because I missed practice last Friday, right? But she can't do that! She told me it was okay just this once . . ."

"Katie, it's not 'Brigadoon,' " Kimmie interrupted quietly. "It's Scott."

"Scott?" Katie stared at her. "What do you mean? There's nothing wrong with him—I spoke to him after class this morning and he looked perfectly fine, although he acted kind of peculiar." Then she had another awful thought. "Is it his grandmother? Did his grandmother have a relapse and die over the weekend?"

Kimmie shook her head. "No. It's not *just* Scott. It's Scott and . . ." She took a deep breath. "Melissa."

Now totally confused and at the end of what little patience she had left, Katie said, "What does Melissa have to do with it? Kimmie, I am sick to death of playing Twenty Questions. Either you tell me what you're talking about, or you can eat lunch all by yourself from now on!"

"Okay, here goes." Kimmie swallowed hard. "Remember Ted's party that Scott invited you to, the one on Saturday night? The one you couldn't go to because you were visiting your aunt in New York?"

Katie nodded.

"Well, Scott went."

"So what? Just because we're going steady doesn't mean he can't go stag to a party when I'm not available," Katie said.

"He didn't go stag. He took Melissa," Kimmie told her.

Katie's immediate reaction was anger and jealousy. But then, remembering that on

123

that same night she herself had been with another guy, she stifled it, saying, "So? We're friends, all three of us. Why shouldn't he take her?"

Instead of answering directly, Kimmie said, "Katie, I know you and Melissa go back a long way, and you know I'm not crazy about her. But I was at that party, and believe me, I heard what I heard and I saw what I saw. So did a lot of your other *real* friends."

Even though the noisy cafeteria was overheated, Katie felt a sudden chill. The bite of tuna sandwich she had just taken stuck in her throat, and she washed it down with a sip of milk. "And?" she managed to say.

"And Melissa told everybody, Scott included, that the reason you couldn't come to the party wasn't because you were spending the whole weekend with your aunt. She said you had a date with a cadet at West Point. Did you, Katie?"

Katie was so shaken that at first she couldn't speak. "Yes," she whispered at last, "I did. I wanted to tell Scott about it because it was only Danny's roommate, but Melissa said I shouldn't because he wouldn't understand and it would hurt his feelings, so I didn't. I didn't even tell you."

"Well, after that announcement your good friend Melissa was all over Scott like ivy on a monument," Kimmie said dryly. "He didn't seem to mind much, either. Carol told me that when she and her date left, they saw Scott and Melissa making out in Scott's car. And on Sunday somebody saw them doing the same thing at Shadow Lake."

Suddenly Katie felt so sick that she was sure she would throw up. But she didn't. She just sat there, staring at her tray and her tuna sandwich.

"Katie?" Kimmie said at last. "Are you okay? Are you mad at me because I told you all this stuff?"

"No," Katie mumbled. "I'm not okay, but I'm not mad—not at you, anyway. You did the right thing. It's not your fault that it happened. I guess if it's anyone's fault, it's mine. If I had been honest with Scott in the first place, maybe it wouldn't have. Happened, I mean. Or maybe it would have eventually . . ."

"So what are you going to do?" Kimmie asked.

"I don't know. I just don't know," Katie whispered.

There was a lump in her throat that felt as big as a grapefruit, and hot tears stung her eyes. But she refused to cry, not here in the cafeteria where everyone could see her. *Remember, Katie Jean O'Connor, you come from a long line of soldiers,* she said to herself, *and soldiers are tough. So what if your heart is breaking? You mustn't let it show.*

Squaring her slumped shoulders, she sat up straight and said loudly enough for anyone who was eavesdropping to hear, "Well, thanks for all the interesting news, Kimmie. Now let me tell you about my weekend. I wish you could have seen Aunt Sheila in that play. She was so good, and the show was so funny! I've never laughed so hard in my whole life . . ."

Somehow Katie managed to rattle on for the rest of the lunch period and to hold her head high during her afternoon classes. It was only when she was heading for the parking lot at the end of the day that she felt her iron self-control crumbling. At the sight of Scott waiting in his car, the misery Katie had been suppressing overwhelmed her, and she almost turned and ran in the opposite direction.

But she didn't. Instead she walked right

126

up to the car. As she got in, Katie could swear there was still a trace of Melissa's French perfume in the air, and she almost gagged. Neither Katie nor Scott said a word. The minute she fastened her seatbelt, he turned the key in the ignition and began to drive.

A few minutes later as they were passing a little park, Katie broke the tense silence. "Stop here, please," she said, staring straight ahead.

Scott didn't look at her either. "I thought you wanted to go to Shadow Lake."

"Not anymore."

He pulled over to the curb and cut the engine. "So what did you want to talk to me about?" Scott asked without turning his head.

Clenching her fists so tightly that her nails dug into her palms, Katie tried to keep her voice from trembling. "Nothing you don't already know. Just for the record, I was going to tell you that after I saw Aunt Sheila's play last weekend, I went to West Point for a blind date with my brother Danny's roommate. I was even going to apologize for not telling you about it when Danny first invited me—"

"So why didn't you?" Scott cut in, looking at her for the first time. His blue eyes were as cold as steel. "That was some stunt you pulled, Katie! Do you have any idea what a jerk I felt like when I found out that my girlfriend—my *steady* girlfriend—was dating another guy? I could hardly believe it when Melissa told me."

"Scott, I wanted to tell you," Katie said. "The reason I didn't was because Melissa convinced me not to. She said it was really an event, not a date, but you'd never understand that and your feelings would be hurt."

"Really?" Scott raised his eyebrows. "Funny—that's not what Melissa told *me*. As a matter of fact, she said it was exactly the other way around. *She* was the one who tried to persuade you to tell me the truth and *you* were the one who wanted to keep this big date a secret."

"And you believed her?" Katie asked incredulously. Scott didn't reply. "You can't possibly still believe her, now that you've heard my side of the story!"

When Scott remained silent, the tears Katie had held back for so long began trickling down her cheeks. "You do, don't you?"

128

she whispered. "Oh, Scott, how could you? I thought we had something really special between us. You said you loved me! How could you cheat on me with my best friend the minute my back was turned? How could you do that to me? To *us*?"

Scott squirmed uncomfortably in his seat. "Look, Katie, I didn't mean for this to happen. But you've been so busy lately, and Melissa was—well, she was so warm and sympathetic. She was always *there*, you know? Melissa was lonely and so was I, and I guess things just kind of got out of control."

"I guess they did," Katie agreed dismally. "By the way, I didn't see her in school today. Did she stay home because she was afraid to face me?"

"Come on, Katie, that's not fair!" Scott said. "It so happens that she woke up this morning with a really bad headache. She gets these migraines sometimes. And anyway, why should Melissa be afraid to face you? It isn't as though this whole thing is her fault, or mine either. You talk about cheating. Who sneaked off to West Point to date some hotshot cadet behind *my* back?"

"Scott, I admit that was wrong, but—"

Full of self-righteous indignation, Scott wouldn't let her finish. "Who made me look like a fool in front of all our friends at Ted's party?"

Furious now, Katie shot back, "My ex–best friend Melissa, that's who! And if you really *do* believe her lies, then all I can say is the two of you deserve each other!"

Flinging open the door, Katie got out of the car. Half blinded by tears of mingled rage and pain, she ran stumbling into the park. Scott didn't follow her.

It was a long walk home, and by the time Katie got there, she was sure she had no more tears to shed. Fortunately both her mother and Willie were out so she didn't have to explain why her face was all red and puffy and her eyes were almost swollen shut. All Katie wanted was to creep upstairs to her room and hide there forever. But first she had something important to do.

She went into the den, closing the door behind her, and dialed Melissa's private number. The phone rang four times before her answering machine kicked in. At the beep after the message, Katie said very clearly and distinctly, "Melissa, this is Katie. I don't believe you're not there. If you don't pick up right now, I'm going to keep calling every five minutes until you do."

A moment later, Melissa answered. "Hi, Katie," she said in a perfectly normal voice. "What's up?"

"Oh, not a whole lot," Katie replied between clenched teeth. "Nothing that you don't know about already, that is. I imagine you even know that Scott and I just broke up, right? Did he give you that news flash by phone, or did he deliver it in person?"

After a brief silence, Melissa said, "Actually, he called a few minutes ago. He's really awfully upset about it, Katie."

Katie could hardly believe her ears. "*He's* upset? Give me a break! How do you think *I* feel about being stabbed in the back by my former boyfriend and my former best friend?"

"Oh, Katie, don't be so melodramatic," Melissa said with a sigh. "You and Scott are all wrong for each other—I realized that after I'd seen the two of you together a few times."

"And now I suppose you're going to tell me

that by lying to him about me and stealing him from me, you were actually doing me a favor!"

"Well, I wouldn't exactly say that," Melissa replied. "But face it, Katie. If Scott was really in love with you, it wouldn't matter what I said or did."

"So you mean that Scott's in love with *you* now?" Katie asked, twisting the phone cord into a knot.

"He thinks he is," Melissa said calmly, "just like he thought he was in love with you."

"Are you in love with him?"

A pause. "Actually, I doubt it. But that's not very important."

"Feelings don't matter to you at all, do they, Melissa?" Katie said in genuine wonder. "Not Scott's, not mine, and not even your own. You've changed so much. I don't think you *have* any feelings anymore! You just like to play games with people, and then drop them when you get bored."

"You're wrong about my not having feelings, Katie," Melissa said very seriously. "I do, but I've discovered that if you let yourself get emotionally involved—with guys, with friends, even with your family—you're just laying yourself open to a whole lot of grief. So I play games instead." She gave an artificial little laugh. "You should try it sometime. It's way more fun!"

"I could never be that way, and I don't really understand how you can either, so I guess I'll just have to take your word for it," Katie said. "Good-bye, Melissa. Have a nice life."

As she slowly hung up the phone, Katie almost felt sorry for Melissa. But she felt a whole lot sorrier for herself.

Chapter Eleven

Katie spent the rest of that afternoon in her room, wallowing in misery. When Willie banged on her door to tell her supper was ready, she said she wasn't feeling well. A few minutes later, both Colonel and Mrs. O'Connor came in to see what was wrong, and between sobs Katie poured out the whole ugly story.

"Oh, honey, I'm so sorry," her mother said, putting her arms around Katie. "Whoever would have guessed that Melissa Harris would turn out to be such a snake in the grass!"

Her father patted her awkwardly on the

134

back, then handed her a tissue. "I never trusted that boy," he said. "Obviously I was right about him all along."

Katie sighed and blew her nose. "It's not really Scott's fault, Dad," she said. "If I'd told him the truth about my trip up front, we might have had an argument, but I'm sure we could have worked things out somehow. Now I've lost him forever, and my best friend, too!"

"In my opinion, it's just as well," her mother said. "Neither of them is worth one single tear. And remember, Katie, Scott McAllister isn't the only boy in the world. What about that nice young cadet you dated at the Point? From what you told us when you got back yesterday, the two of you had a good time. Perhaps if you visited your brother again soon . . ."

"Mom, you don't understand!" Katie wailed. "Ben and I *did* have a good time, but he could never take Scott's place. Even though he dumped me, I'm still in love with Scott."

Colonel O'Connor shook his head. "I'm sure your mother *does* understand, and I also think she's absolutely right. Forget about Scott and Melissa and get on with your life. That's an order," he added with a slight smile.

But forgetting about them was easier said than done. The news of Katie's breakup with Scott had spread through Hillwood High like wildfire, and it seemed that everywhere Katie looked, she saw Scott and Melissa, the golden couple. Melissa never said a word to her, and in World Lit, Scott ignored her completely.

Although Katie kept smiling until her face ached, pretending she didn't care, Kimmie and her other loyal friends knew how much she was hurting inside. They treated her with tender concern, as though she had some dreadful illness that everyone knew about but nobody dared to mention, and it drove her crazy.

The only bright spot during that awful time was "Brigadoon." The musical was scheduled to open in a little less than three weeks, and Ms. Carletti had scheduled rehearsals not only after school each day, but on weekends as well.

That was fine with Katie—she had nothing better to do since she and Scott had broken up. In fact, she could hardly wait until she could escape into the magic world of the little village that emerged from the Scottish mists only once every hundred years.

Immersing herself in the role of Fiona MacClaren and her romance with Tommy Albright, Katie was able to put her own shattered romance out of her mind for hours at a time. She was letter-perfect in her part and practiced Fiona's songs at home whenever she had a spare minute. Katie's performance improved so much that Ms. Carletti, who was very hard to please, actually complimented her several times.

As long as she was surrounded by her fellow Thespians, Katie felt almost normal. Unlike her other friends, they were far more interested in making the show a success than in school gossip. Even when Katie joined other members of the cast and stage crew at the local hangout for a snack after rehearsals, all anyone ever talked about was "Brigadoon."

But no matter how much she rehearsed or how hard she worked in school and at home to keep up with her studies, sooner or later Katie found her thoughts drifting back to how happy she had been with Scott before beautiful, glamorous, treacherous Melissa entered the picture.

Lying in bed each night, she remembered how often he had said, "I love you," and how completely she had believed him. She knew Scott was saying the same thing to Melissa, and the thought made Katie bury her face in her pillow to muffle her sobs.

In spite of how much he's hurt me, I'll never stop loving him, never, never, never, she vowed night after night as she cried herself to sleep.

Saturday's rehearsal was long and grueling, and Katie was exhausted when Carol dropped her off at home late that afternoon. Her throat was scratchy from singing so much and her legs ached from dancing for hours. Katie was looking forward to soaking in a hot, scented bubble bath, but she was *not* looking forward to the pile of homework that awaited her. *Saturday nights sure aren't what they used to be,* she thought gloomily.

"I'm home," she called as she hung up her jacket in the hall closet.

Mrs. O'Connor came out of the kitchen. "Hi, honey. How did it go today?"

Katie shrugged. "Okay, I guess. Frankly, I'm too tired to tell. If I never see another piece of heather again it'll be too soon!"

"Poor baby. I know this show is very important to you, but I think you're working much too hard. I was just fixing myself a cup of herb tea. Want one?" her mother asked.

"Sure," Katie said. "And could you put some honey in it? My throat's kind of sore."

Mrs. O'Connor frowned. "I hope you're not coming down with something."

"I'll be fine, Mom," Katie assured her. "I'm pooped and a little grumpy, that's all."

"Well, take a look on the hall table," her mother said with a mysterious smile as she went back into the kitchen. "There's a letter for you. Maybe it will cheer you up."

Going over to the table, Katie saw a familiar gray envelope with the West Point crest. Surprised to be hearing from Danny so soon after her visit, she opened it without paying attention to the handwriting on the front.

Katie was even more surprised to discover that the letter wasn't from her brother at all—it was from Ben Anderson.

Dear Katie, she read.

Greetings from Martian Cadet Anderson, who wants to thank you for a day that was out of this world!

I was trying to be funny so I could make you smile, but I really mean that. I also want to tell you again how sorry I am about coming on to you the way I did last Saturday night. I hope you're not mad at me, and that we can be friends. Would you mind if I write to you sometimes? You don't have to answer this letter, but I sure would like it if you did.

> *Yours truly,*
> *Ben Anderson*
> *Company D-1*

Katie was smiling as she tucked the letter into her jeans pocket and joined her mother in the kitchen.

"So what did Ben have to say?" Mrs. O'Connor asked, then added hastily, "Of course, you don't have to tell me if you don't want to, and I certainly don't mean to pry. But I couldn't help noticing that the letter wasn't from Danny, and . . ."

"It's okay, Mom. Relax," Katie said. "Ben

didn't divulge any military secrets or anything. He just said he enjoyed our date, and asked if I'd mind if he wrote to me every now and then."

"I see." Her mother handed her a mug of steaming herb tea. "And do you? Mind, I mean?"

"Why should I?" Katie said casually after she took a sip. "It's a free country. He can write to anybody he wants to."

"I hope you'll answer his letters, dear," Mrs. O'Connor said. "You never can tell where something like this may lead. I'll never forget the love letters your father and I used to write to each other while he was at West Point."

Katie groaned. "*Please*, Mom! This isn't the same thing at all. You and Dad were practically engaged, but I hardly even *know* Ben Anderson."

"True," her mother agreed. "But corresponding with someone is an excellent way to find out what that person is really like. And now that you're no longer involved with Scott . . ."

"Mom, Scott dumped me for Melissa less than two weeks ago," Katie pointed out wearily. "It's going to be a very long time—maybe *years*—before I get over that, if I ever do. And even then, I'm sure I'll never trust another guy again."

She carried her mug of tea out of the kitchen and trudged upstairs. When she took off her jeans, getting ready for her bubble bath, Katie took Ben's letter out of the pocket. As she read it for the second time, an image formed in her mind of his pleasant, friendly face, with its twinkling brown eyes and crooked smile. He'd looked so silly when he did his "alien" impersonation!

But Ben hadn't looked silly at all when he kissed her. Remembering how she had responded to that kiss, if only for a second, Katie felt guilty all over again. *I never should have let him kiss me,* she said to herself. *And if I'd told him I was going steady with somebody back home, he never would have done it. Ben's not the kind of guy who'd kiss another guy's girl. He's too honest, not like . . .*

Katie didn't let herself finish that thought. Wrapping her robe around her, she headed for the bathroom and began running hot water into the tub. As she added her favorite lilac-scented bubble bath, Katie admitted that she hadn't been fair to Ben by allowing him to think she was available when she wasn't. *I guess I really ought to answer his letter and explain so he can stop blaming himself for something that wasn't his fault,* she thought.

After an hour-long soak that soothed Katie's aches and pains, she put on her comfortable old sweatpants and one of her father's cast-off flannel shirts. Then, before she could change her mind, she sat down at her desk and began to write:

Dear Ben,

Thanks for your letter. I never got one from a Martian before! Also, thanks for a great time at the Point. I really enjoyed all the things we did together.

I'm not mad at you for kissing me. I acted the way I did because at the time, I was going steady with a boy here at Benning. I should have told you that when we first met, but I didn't. I'm telling you now because you're very nice and I don't want you to feel bad about it anymore.

Sincerely,

Katie

She addressed the envelope and put it in her purse to mail in the morning, then opened her history book. But though she tried to concentrate on her homework assignment, Katie couldn't help wondering how Ben would react to her letter, and if he would write to her again.

Chapter Twelve

The next five days before the "Brigadoon" opening on Friday night were so hectic that in comparison, the previous weeks seemed almost peaceful. In addition to rehearsals after school each day, Katie had a history exam on Tuesday and a physics exam on Wednesday. The technical rehearsal on Wednesday afternoon went off without a hitch, but at dress rehearsal the following night disaster struck. Katie couldn't believe all the things that went wrong!

To begin with, she couldn't find one of the shoes that went with her costume, so she had to wear her sneakers for her first entrance. As soon as she came onstage, Ms. Carletti had a fit, rattling Katie so much that she completely forgot her lines.

But Katie wasn't the only one who had problems. All the dancers suddenly seemed to have developed two left feet and the singers in the chorus were off-key. Jim Rhodes, who played Tommy Albright, Fiona's love interest, was fighting a cold and sneezed all the way through their romantic scenes. A piece of scenery—fortunately a small one—fell on Carol's head, and the lamp in the follow spot blew.

Most spectacular of all, the mist machine that the Thespians had borrowed from a Little Theater group in Columbus went completely haywire, spewing out such thick fog that in a matter of minutes none of the actors onstage could see each other.

"Heathcliff! Heathcliff! Come back to Wuthering Heights!" someone wailed mournfully, and everybody, even Ms. Carletti, broke up.

One of the stagehands managed to fix the machine, and as the mist began to clear, the rehearsal continued without too many more mishaps. When the curtain closed on the last act, the frazzled cast and crew gathered onstage for a final word from Ms. Carletti.

"Well, boys and girls," she said, "as you all know, there's an old saying in the theater that a bad dress rehearsal means a good performance. I certainly hope that's true, because considering how this rehearsal went, tomorrow night's performance ought to be the best that Hillwood High has ever seen!" After the laughter had died down, she went on, "Seriously, kids, you've all done a terrific job, and I know that in spite of all that went wrong tonight, 'Brigadoon' is going to be a huge success. Now I want all of you to go straight home and get a good night's sleep so you'll be fresh and rested for our opening."

When Katie walked in the door of her house half an hour later, she was still so keyed up that she didn't feel tired at all. Hearing the sound of the television coming from the den, she found her parents there watching a documentary. She was just about to give them a blow-by-blow account of everything that had happened that evening when her father said, "Before I forget, Katie, you got a phone call while you were out."

"Really?" Katie couldn't imagine who might have phoned since all her friends at school knew she'd be at dress rehearsal.

"Yes, honey." Mrs. O'Connor beamed at her. "Ben Anderson called a couple of hours ago. Your father told him about the play, and Ben said he'd call back around ten."

Katie was amazed. Why had Ben phoned? What on earth did he want to talk to her about? Glancing at the clock on the fireplace mantel, she saw that it was twenty after ten.

"Well, I guess he must have changed his mind," she said. "Now let me tell you about tonight's rehearsal. I never saw such a mess in my entire life! In the first place, I couldn't find one of my shoes—"

Just then the phone rang.

"You might as well answer it, Katie," Colonel O'Connor said. "It's probably Ben."

Mrs. O'Connor stood up. "Yes, Katie, why don't you answer it while your father and I go into the kitchen for some ice cream. You were just saying that you felt like having some ice cream, weren't you, dear?" she said to her husband.

"Ice cream?" Katie's father looked at her

mother as though she'd gone mad. "You know I never eat ice cream, particularly not in the middle of November!"

"There's a first time for everything," Mrs. O'Connor said. Taking his hand, she pulled him up from the couch. "And I think Katie deserves some privacy, don't you?"

As the door closed behind them, Katie counted the rings of the phone. On the tenth ring, she picked up the receiver.

"Hello?"

"Katie? This is Ben—Cadet Ben Anderson of Company D-1, roommate of your brother Cadet Danny O'Connor, in case you've forgotten."

At the sound of his Montana drawl, Katie couldn't help smiling. "The only Ben Anderson I know comes from outer space," she said. "He's from the western part of the planet Mars."

"That's me. I only reveal my true identity to very special people like you." After a brief pause, Ben said, "Katie, I got your letter today, and I just have one question. You said that when you came to West Point, you were going steady with a guy back home. Although you didn't say it in so many words, I got the impression that you weren't going steady with him anymore. Is that correct?"

Katie swallowed hard. "Yes. We broke up when I found out he'd been seeing my best friend while I was away."

"Fantastic!" Ben exclaimed. "I mean, I guess you're pretty wrecked about it right now, but—well, I was wondering if maybe you'd keep on writing to me whenever you have the time. Like a friend, you know? I wouldn't make any demands on you or anything. What do you say?"

Katie couldn't think of any reason to refuse, so she said, "Okay. Like a friend. But don't expect too many letters—Danny's probably told you what a lousy correspondent I am."

"You're right, he has," Ben said cheerfully. "That's all right with me. Listen, Katie, tell me about this play you're in. I didn't know you were an actress. In fact, I don't really know much about you at all."

"Well, I wouldn't exactly call myself an actress," Katie said modestly. "I mean, that's not what I plan to do for a career, but I love to act, and I can sing and dance a little. I'm playing the lead in our school production of 'Brigadoon.' We open tomorrow night. It's a musical about this little magic village in Scotland, and—"

"Oh, I know 'Brigadoon,' " Ben interrupted. "When my folks took me to New York once about three years ago, we saw it. I'd never been to a Broadway show before, and it really blew me away."

Katie cried, "You saw that production? Then you must have seen my aunt, Sheila Sheridan—she played Fiona, the same part I'm playing now. I stayed with Aunt Sheila and saw her new play the night before I went to West Point, and then she drove me up there on Saturday morning."

"No kidding!" Ben sounded really impressed. "I never met anybody who was related to a Broadway star before!"

"Yes, you did," Katie said, giggling. "My brother Danny! He's related to Aunt Sheila too, you know."

"Well, I'll be darned. I'd sure like to meet her some time, maybe even get her autograph for my mom," Ben said. "Mom loved 'Brigadoon.' She's crazy about the theater, but she hardly ever gets to go because she and Dad are stuck out there on our ranch in the middle of nowhere."

"What's it like, living on a ranch?" Katie asked. "My family has lived in a lot of different places, but we've never been out west."

Ben was only too happy to tell her about the wide open spaces he called home, and Katie listened, so fascinated by what he had to say that she was amazed when the mantel clock chimed eleven times.

"Ben, if you're calling from a pay phone, this must be costing you a fortune," she said. "I'd love to hear more about your ranch, but I think we'd better hang up now."

"I guess you're right," he agreed. "I didn't mean to bend your ear for so long. I'll tell you the rest in my next letter, okay? And Katie, good luck with your show tomorrow night. I wish I could be there to see it."

Katie said, "I wish you could, too," and realized to her surprise that she meant it. Then, smiling, she added, "By the way, for your information, it's *bad* luck to wish an actor good luck with a performance. You're supposed to say 'break a leg.' "

Ben laughed. "Now *that* is really weird!

Okay then, break a leg, Katie. Sleep tight, and write to me real soon."

"Night, Ben. Thanks for calling, and give my love to that big brother of mine."

As Katie hung up the phone and went up-, stairs to bed, she was happier than she'd felt in weeks.

On Friday evening as Katie and the other girls in the cast of "Brigadoon" were getting into costume and putting on their makeup in the crowded, noisy dressing room, three florist's boxes were delivered to her. One contained a huge arrangement of blossoms from her parents, Willie, and Danny. Though Aunt Sheila would be unable to come to the show because the run of her play had been extended, she had sent a dozen long-stemmed American Beauty roses with a loving note.

"Who's that one from, Katie?" Carol asked eagerly as Katie opened the last box and took out a nosegay of tiny pink sweetheart roses and baby's breath.

"I haven't the slightest idea," Katie said, rummaging through the green tissue paper.

"There doesn't seem to be any card. Maybe it's from Kimmie." But she couldn't help thinking sadly that this was the kind of bouquet that Scott would have sent, if only. . . .

"Here's the card," Alison, one of the dancers, said, handing her a small white envelope. "It must have fallen on the floor."

Katie opened it and read the brief message inside: "Break a leg, Katie. This alien is rooting for you." It was unsigned, but she knew perfectly well who had sent it.

Peering over her shoulder, Carol said, "Alien? What on earth does that mean?"

"Private joke," Katie said, grinning. For the past few hours, she had been fighting a bad case of opening-night jitters, but suddenly she felt confident and serene. Tonight Katie Jean O'Connor was going to give the performance of her life!

And she did. So did everybody else—all the problems that had plagued them the night before magically disappeared. Voices rang out clear and true on the musical numbers, the dancers were all in step, Jim didn't sneeze even once, and the mist machine behaved itself beautifully. The auditorium was packed, and the audience applauded so long

154

and hard at the end that the cast took seven curtain calls.

"Congratulations to every single one of you," Ms. Carletti said after their final bows. "You were just as brilliant as I knew you'd be. Now all you have to do is keep it up for three more performances!"

Katie quickly took off her stage makeup and exchanged her costume for her street clothes, then gathered up her three bouquets. As she hurried out of the building to meet her parents and Willie, Kimmie and several of her other friends came up to her, raving about how good she was. Katie felt as if she were walking on air. *Maybe I'll decide on a career in the theater after all,* she thought as she ran down the front steps of the school.

Katie's head was so full of dreams that she didn't notice Scott and Melissa until she almost bumped into them at the bottom of the steps. For what seemed like an eternity, the three of them stood staring at each other.

At last Melissa broke the awkward silence. "Great performance, Katie," she said with a dazzling smile. "You were absolutely terrific, much better than I would have been."

"Thanks," Katie replied stiffly.

"You really were good, Katie," Scott mumbled. "Congratulations."

He looked so nervous and uncomfortable! What did he expect her to do? Katie wondered. Burst into tears? Beg him to come back to her? Attack him and Melissa in a fit of jealous rage? Katie had a sudden almost irresistible urge to laugh, and at that very moment she realized to her astonishment that the impossible had happened. Without being aware of it, she had stopped being madly in love with Scott. She wasn't even angry at Melissa anymore.

The smile Katie gave them both over her armful of flowers was even more dazzling than Melissa's had been. "I'm so glad you enjoyed the show," she said. "I'd love to stay and chat, but I really have to run—my family's waiting to take me out for an opening night celebration. Well, guess I'll see you around."

Then Katie turned and walked briskly toward the parking lot. She wasn't tempted to look back, not even once.

Chapter Thirteen

"Brigadoon" played to packed houses every performance of its weekend run, proving to be the most successful show the Thespians had ever presented. In the days that followed, Katie, like all the other members of the cast and crew, suffered from the usual case of post-production letdown. After so many weeks of total immersion in the fantasy world of the musical, it was hard to come back down to earth. Without lines to learn, songs to practice, and rehearsals every day after school, Katie suddenly found herself with more time on her hands than she knew what to do with.

But not for long. On Wednesday while Katie was waiting for Kimmie to come through the cafeteria line, Johnnie Warden came over to her and began insisting that she return to "Teen Scene" on a regular basis. According to Johnnie's own personal survey of the Hillwood High student body, the radio show had been losing listeners since Katie had stopped appearing on the program.

"The kids really miss your fashion commentary and those movie and music reviews you used to do," he told her. "And we got a terrific response to your interview with Melissa Harris—" Johnnie broke off abruptly, obviously embarrassed. "Uh, sorry, Katie—I guess I shouldn't have brought that up, considering . . ."

"Considering what?" Katie said calmly. "You mean because Melissa stole my boyfriend?" Johnnie shrugged and nodded. "Don't worry about it, okay? It still makes me sad sometimes when I remember how close Melissa and I used to be, and how much I cared for Scott, but I'm not all bent out of shape anymore, honest."

"I'm glad, Katie," he said, smiling. "*Really

glad. And now that you're back in circulation, there's something else I wanted to ask you. I thought maybe—well, I've always liked you a lot, and I was wondering if you'd like to go out with me some time."

Katie sighed. "Oh, Johnnie, I like you a lot, too, but I'm afraid I'm not ready to start dating again just yet. I'll always be your friend, though, and I'll be happy to do some shows with you."

Johnnie looked so disappointed that Katie felt sorry for him. When she saw Kimmie walking toward them with her tray, she had a sudden inspiration. "Why don't you have lunch with Kimmie and me?" she suggested. "We can talk about 'Teen Scene' while we eat."

He agreed, and after Katie and Johnnie discussed her participation in future programs, Katie managed to steer the conversation around to movies, knowing both her friends were crazy about classic old films. Soon Kimmie and Johnnie were talking nonstop, and from the sparkle in Kimmie's eyes and the smile on Johnnie's face, Katie could tell that Johnnie hadn't been too badly hurt by her refusal to date him. When she finished her lunch, he and Kimmie were so absorbed in each other that neither of them even noticed when Katie picked up her tray and left the table.

That evening, Kimmie phoned to say that she and Johnnie were going to the movies on Saturday night. "I can't believe he asked me out!" she said. "I've always kind of admired Johnnie from afar—I never miss a single 'Teen Scene' program because I just love the sound of his voice. You don't mind, do you, Katie?" she added anxiously.

Katie laughed. "Why should I mind?"

"Well, you and Johnnie were always pretty tight, and now that you're not dating Scott anymore, I just thought . . ." Her voice trailed off.

"Johnnie's one of the nicest guys I know," Katie said, "but that's as far as it goes. I'm happy for you both, Kimmie. I think the two of you would make a great couple."

Kimmie heaved a sigh of relief. "Oh, good! I just didn't want you to think I was pulling a Melissa!" She paused, then said softly, "Katie, how are you doing? I mean, since you and Scott broke up. You haven't said much about it at all."

"I'm doing pretty well, all things considered," Katie said. "In fact, I'm doing a lot better than I thought I would. I thought my heart was broken, but I guess it was only cracked."

"So you put a Band-Aid on it, right?" Kimmie joked.

"Something like that." Thinking about the bouquet of pink sweetheart roses and baby's breath in a vase in her bedroom, Katie smiled. "And a certain West Point cadet has been giving me a lot of long-distance therapy."

"Oh, Katie!" Kimmie exclaimed. "That's so great! Are you going to see him again?"

"I don't know. Ben and I write to each other, and we've talked on the phone, but—well, I just don't know."

"Well, when you *do* know, let me in on it, okay?" Kimmie urged, and Katie promised she would.

Over the next few weeks, Katie and Ben exchanged many letters and phone calls in which they discovered a great deal about each other. Everything Katie learned about Ben made her like him more. When Danny came home for Thanksgiving, he hand-delivered a note from Ben, inviting Katie to West Point the first weekend in December.

"No football game this time," Ben wrote, "but there's an ice-skating party Saturday afternoon, and a chili supper hosted by Colonel Travis, one of my professors. He's from Texas, and his chili is guaranteed to make you thirsty for at least a year. If you wear those false eyelashes, it'll probably burn them right off! We could have a lot of fun, Katie. Please say yes."

"I see no reason why you shouldn't go," Colonel O'Connor said when Katie told her parents about Ben's invitation. "It so happens that I'll be going to the Point that weekend on business—could be I'll be assigned up there next year. We can go together, Katie, if you don't mind flying with your crusty old dad."

Katie didn't mind at all. After persuading Kimmie to cover for her on the "Teen Scene" broadcast she'd miss, Katie sent a note back with Danny, accepting Ben's invitation and relaying her father's request that Ben and Danny join them for breakfast that Saturday morning. As soon as Ben received her reply, he phoned to tell her how much he was looking forward to her visit.

"And bring plenty of warm clothes," he added. "It's been snowing like crazy up here."

"Snow!" Katie cried in delight. "Oh, I can hardly wait! I haven't seen snow in years!"

"I can hardly wait to see *you*," Ben said. "If I'd known how you feel about snow, I'd have had my folks send me a truckload from Montana weeks ago. Then maybe I could have lured you up here sooner!"

Late the following Friday afternoon, Katie was on her way to West Point again. But this time she felt no guilt, only anticipation. Also, there was no longer any tension between herself and her father. On the flight to New York, Colonel O'Connor never once said "I told you so," but he made no secret of the fact that he heartily approved of this new young man in his daughter's life.

At LaGuardia airport, they transferred to a rental car. As her father drove north in the deepening twilight, Katie was thrilled by the rugged, snow-covered landscape. It had begun to snow again when they reached the Thayer Hotel, and while her father went into the lobby to check on their reservations, she remained outside for a few minutes, savoring the icy caress of snowflakes on her flushed cheeks.

This is so wonderful, Katie thought happily. But she knew as she entered the hotel that it wasn't just the wintery weather that filled her with excitement. The prospect of seeing Cadet Ben Anderson of Company D-1 the next day had a great deal to do with it.

Promptly at ten o'clock the next morning, Ben and Danny arrived at the Thayer. Katie and her father were waiting for them in the lobby, and as the two cadets approached, Katie's heart gave a funny little skip. Ben was so much more handsome than she had remembered! But what was Ben thinking as he looked at her? she wondered nervously. She had taken great care with her appearance, but what if he didn't like what he saw? What if she was homelier than he remembered? What if he was sorry he'd asked her to come?

Feeling intensely shy and awkward, Katie gave her brother a kiss, then turned to Ben. Unsure of how to greet him, after a moment's hesitation, she decided on a friendly handshake. She stuck out her hand, and as Ben's cold fingers touched Katie's, a spark of static electricity made them both jump.

Grinning at her, he said, "It sure is a real *shock* seeing you again, Katie!"

She giggled. Suddenly she wasn't nervous anymore—Ben's silly joke and the admiration in his warm brown eyes made her shyness melt away. Danny introduced him to Colonel O'Connor, and the four of them went into the Thayer's elegantly old-fashioned dining room. As they ate a huge, delicious breakfast, Katie said very little. She just sat and listened while her father and the boys talked shop about the military academy, glad that Ben seemed to be making a good impression on the colonel.

After their meal, Katie's father announced that he was going to visit an old army friend. "What about you young people?" he asked Katie and Ben. "I know about the skating party and the chili supper later today, but what do you plan to do until then?"

Katie glanced questioningly at Ben, who said, "Well, sir, the last time your daughter was here, I started to give her a guided tour of the Point, but we got started pretty late, and then it began to rain so she didn't get to see very much. I thought we'd give it another shot this morning, maybe take a look at Fort Putnam." Smiling at Katie, he added, "Unless you'd rather not plow through all this snow you're so crazy about, that is."

"Oh, no, I'd love it!" Katie assured him. "I even brought boots and a really warm parka just in case."

"Well, run up to your room and put them on then," Colonel O'Connor said. "I'm dropping Danny off at Grant Hall, and if you and Ben are going to Fort Putnam, I'll drop you there as well. It's much too far to walk from here."

"Thanks, Dad. Be back in a flash."

After Katie had bundled up, they all piled into her father's rental car. It wasn't until Danny had gone inside Grant Hall and Colonel O'Connor had driven away that Katie and Ben were on their own at last.

"Lead on, Cadet Anderson," she said, saluting him with one mittened hand.

"It's kind of a long walk and mostly uphill. Are you sure you're up to this?" Ben asked.

"I don't want you to get so worn out that you won't be able to skate this afternoon."

Katie grinned at him. "I'm a lot tougher than I look. Besides, it's a gorgeous day for sightseeing. I wish I'd brought my sunglasses, though—the sunlight on all that snow is almost blinding."

With a mock scowl, Ben said, "Is that a complaint, Miss O'Connor? You wanted snow, I ordered snow. If you *didn't* want sunshine, you should have told me."

"Sorry about that," Katie said with a giggle. "It's very nice sunshine, really. Now are we going to see this fort, or are we going to stand here and turn into icicles?"

"We're on our way."

Ben tucked her arm through his and they began trudging along, Katie taking two steps to each of Ben's one. They passed several other cadets and their dates, but nobody else seemed to be going in the same direction.

"Are you sure Fort Putnam is this way?" Katie puffed as they ascended the snow-covered hill.

"It is unless they moved it during the

night," Ben said. "Patience, Katie. We're al-most there."

Not long afterward, he gestured toward an old fort off to their right. "See? I told you. That's Fort Putnam. But that's not really what I wanted to show you."

Katie stopped in her tracks. "You've got to be kidding! We came all this way, and we're not even going to *look* at it?"

"We'll look at it later. Come on, Katie. There's something else I want you to see."

With Katie's arm still entwined with his, Ben veered to the left into a wooded area and stopped beneath a gnarled old oak. "Look up there," he directed, pointing at the bare branches above their heads.

Katie looked, and saw a large rock cradled in the cleft of one large limb. Turning back to Ben, she said, "What on earth . . . ?"

"You know about Kissing Rock and Flirta-tion Walk, right?" he said. Katie nodded. "And I guess you also know that plebes aren't allowed to take their dates down Flir-tation Walk until June, when they're finally recognized as human beings by their fellow cadets." Katie nodded again, increasingly puzzled. "Well, June's a long way down the road, and I just couldn't wait until then," Ben went on. "So this is a substitute Kissing Rock."

Katie's eyes widened. "*You* put it up there?"

"Yep. I did it as soon as I knew you were coming."

"You did it for me?"

Putting his gloved hands on her shoulders, Ben said solemnly, "I hope some day we'll go down Flirtation Walk together, Katie. But in the meantime, this will have to do."

"Oh, Ben!" she whispered. "I—I don't know what to say."

"I'd like you to say that you want me to kiss you," he said softly. "I told you the first time you came that I wouldn't unless you said you wanted me to, and I won't. But I care about you a whole lot, more than I ever thought I would. Do you think you could care for me too?"

Katie didn't answer immediately. As she gazed into his sweet, honest eyes, many memories flooded her mind—Scott saying, "I love you, Katie." Melissa saying, "It's not really a date, it's an event." Scott and Melissa, the golden couple, and all the pain Katie had felt when they had betrayed her. But that was over now.

"I do care for you, Ben," she murmured. "I'm not in love with you, but I think maybe I could be. And I would like it very much if you would kiss me now."

He pulled her into his arms then, and Ben kissed her and held her as if he never wanted to let her go.